QUEST

Stories of Journeys from around Europe from the Aarhus 39

Edited by Daniel Hahn

International Children's Literature

HAY FESTIVAL

AARHUS 39

*celebrating the best emerging writers for
young people from across wider Europe*

ALMA BOOKS

ALMA BOOKS LTD
3 Castle Yard
Richmond
Surrey TW10 6TF
United Kingdom
www.almabooks.com

Quest first published by Alma Books Ltd in 2017

Original texts © the authors, 2017
Translations © the translators, 2017
Illustrations © the illustrators, 2017
Full credits can be found on the Copyright Information page at the
end of the volume

Introduction © Daniel Hahn, 2017

Printed in Great Britain by CPI Group (UK) Ltd, Croydon CR0 4YY

ISBN: 978-1-84688-426-9

Contents

Introduction

If you're a reader, embarking on a new story is like setting off on a journey. Maybe you think you know in advance where you're headed, or maybe you're happy just to discover the path along the way, one step at a time. What will the road be like? Who will you meet? Will the trip be exciting or dull, funny or frightening – and where will it end? Is it dangerous? Will there be dragons?

Each of the writers in *Quest* is inviting you to go with them on a journey and, as you might expect, each one is quite different. The writers themselves come from fourteen different countries and write in eleven different languages; some write about real places they know well, others invent extraordinary worlds of pure fantasy. In a few of the stories, the border between what's real and what's fantasy might not even be that clear. As you explore the stories in this book, there's really no telling what you may find.

Along the way, you might meet a girl looking for a new name, and talking animals, and imaginary grandparents; or a trio of sleepless sisters, some brave runaways and a Chosen One on a quest. (Just watch out for those Kraiks. They are *nasty*.) Maybe you'll have rooftop adventures and visit mysterious libraries and explore a house full of wonders like you've never imagined, or perhaps there will be a treehouse and time travel and... a very embarrassing Christmas jumper?

There's only one way to find out.

Stories aren't always easy. Oftentimes they ask a great deal of their readers. They ask you to be bold, to take risks, to follow where they lead. To surrender to them. To trust them. Stories ask you to think things you've never thought before. They ask you to be generous, open-hearted and welcoming, to imagine what it's like being a different person in a different world, to imagine just what that feels like. Because while you're inside a story, for those few strange, magical minutes, you could be anyone, anywhere. Being a reader requires a kind of bravery, I've always thought.

In 2017 the Danish city of Aarhus is European Capital of Culture. As part of the celebrations, the Hay Festival and their friends have selected thirty-nine of Europe's best writers for young people – the "Aarhus 39" – and we are excited and proud to have new stories by seventeen of them in this book. The most wonderful stories can come from pretty much anywhere, and wherever they happen to be from, they always love to travel in search of new readers. I hope *Quest* will show you that.

Seventeen journeys, just waiting for you to take a first step...

– Daniel Hahn

Quest

Beware Low-Flying Girls

Katherine Rundell

Odile could fly only when the wind blew.

It was cold, that day she first took flight, and the snow lay thick enough to hide a cat in.

She wore her father's coat. It came down past her knees, and she had rolled the sleeves up, so they hung at her wrist in a great roll of wool. The coat had once been a deep, cocoa-bean brown, but now it was the colour of an elderly shoe. It smelt, very slightly, of horses and woodsmoke.

The wind was fierce that day. It was often windy in winter at the top of the mountain; birds got blown backwards up the cliff edge, reverse-somersaulting through the sky, their wings shedding feathers like confetti. Seagulls blew into the house, sometimes right into her lap as she sat curled up in a corner, wrapped in rugs, reading by the firelight. Suddenly finding that you had an irate seagull as a bookmark was not, Odile thought, ideal, but her grandfather would throw a blanket over them and stomp out into the night with the bird bundled in his arms.

'Always be polite to birds,' he would say. 'They know more than they let on.'

The house was built into the rock of the mountain, and the door was polished stone. Her grandfather had lived on the mountaintop all his life. Odile had lived with him since she was a baby. She had nobody else. In the house, the fire burned all the year round. 'Keep the fire as hot as the human heart,' said her grandfather, his jaw stern. 'Never let it go out.'

That day, she had pulled her father's coat around her, and set out to find what food might still be going – truffles, deep underground, and any nuts the squirrels might have hoarded. She felt a little guilty about the squirrels. Her grandfather always raised his eyebrows over this guilt, because Odile also carried a slingshot in her coat pocket to take a squirrel home for casserole if she could find one.

The wind caught the coat as she walked down the mountain path, billowing it out behind her like a sail. It had no buttons left, so she took a corner of the coat in each fist and held her arms stiff at her side. She began to run, her hair blowing in her eyes and mouth, down the hill.

The wind caught the coat and tossed her upwards. Odile felt the sudden swoop of gravity undone.

It lasted only a second. She screamed, pulling her coat up over her face, and dropped to the ground again, landing on her hands and knees in the snow. Her breathing stopped. Though she had barely fallen two feet, she felt winded, gasping and choking for air.

'I flew,' she whispered. Or had she perhaps just tripped and fallen more extravagantly than usual? She had to be sure.

Odile rubbed some snow into her eyes to make sure she was awake. She pulled a twig from a tree, brushed the frost from it and used it to pin her hair out of her eyes. She put on her gloves.

She stretched out the corners of her coat. She began to run, downhill, her feet kicking up a spray of snow.

The coat billowed out behind her. Her breath misted the air in front of her.

And Odile flew.

She was lifted higher this time, jerking upward with each gust of wind, until she was five feet from the ground, swooping down the hill, her cheeks pushed up and backwards towards her eyebrows and the wind bellowing in her ears.

A cluster of trees rose up ahead of her. She tried to steer left, kicking her right leg against the air. Her rubber boot dislodged and disappeared into the tree's branches, but she found herself lurching sideways, and higher, up above the tops of the trees, buffeting left and right on the back of the wind.

It was pure luck that, when the wind unexpectedly dropped, Odile was up above the treetops, trying not to catch her toes in the upper branches of a circle of oaks. She fell without warning into the tree's embrace. A branch had gouged a red slash out of her chin, but otherwise she was unhurt. She walked back up the mountain to retrieve her fallen boot, her heart racing double-time.

Since that first day, Odile had learnt the mechanics of the wind. She had learnt how to steer, and how to hover, mid-air, her coat billowing around her ears. She had learnt that, if the wind dropped when she was flying high, so did she. So she kept, as best she could, within three or four feet of the ground. The desire to soar upwards was always there. Odile had broken her ankle, but only once, and fractured her wrist twice. It had been the same wrist both times, and her grandfather had been unimpressed.

'You need to take better care of your bones,' he said. He had wrapped her wrist in a wooden splint, and covered it in quilted cotton, which he had sewed himself, squinting cantankerously in the firelight. 'You don't get new ones.' Odile's grandfather, like her father before his death, had been a doctor. The room that was now the kitchen had once been his dispensary.

The coat did not surprise Odile's grandfather. 'Your father used to do it,' he said.

'Papa used to fly too?' Odile felt a glow in her stomach: a glow that was also an ache.

'He did. He was a little older than you. But no wiser. I lost count of the number of times I confiscated that wretched coat. But he always found it again, and I couldn't bring myself to burn it.'

'Please don't burn it!' Odile clutched at her grandfather's wrist.

'Well. There's no point in telling you not to use it, I suppose?'

Odile didn't want to be rude. 'I could lie. If it would help?'

'It would not. But keep it a secret,' he said. 'And stay low. There have been too many stories about people flying, and they never end well. You've heard of Icarus?'

'I'm not going to *melt*, Grandpa!'

'Fine, fine.' He shook his head at her, stern and grey. 'Just stay away from the Kraiks.'

The Kraiks lived in the trees that lined the west peak of the mountainside. They could talk, but that didn't mean you wanted to listen to their conversation. They were birds, of a sort.

'Never listen to a Kraik,' said Odile's grandfather. 'They know things they shouldn't.'

'What?' Odile had asked. It sounded exciting.

'They know your fears, and your secrets,' said Odile's grandfather – which sounded much less so. 'Fears are unwieldy things. They might be nothing more than sleep-spun nightmares, head-dwelling nothings with no real in them, but a Kraik can make them sound like red-blooded truth. It doesn't pay to listen to them.'

The Kraiks would eat whatever they could get: newborn deer in spring, rabbits in summer and badgers in winter. They were unlikely to eat an entire human, but it was not unheard of for them to kill a child and eat an arm, an ear, a foot or two.

Odile gave the west side of the mountain a wide berth when she went to the village school. She was a boarder there from Monday morning until lunchtime on Friday, when she would hike up the mountain again. Or, if there was a wind, she opened her coat and flew, her boots dangling a few feet from the ground, weaving in and out of trees and brushing her ankles against the tops of snow-capped hedgerows.

It was a bright Friday in December, within spitting distance of Christmas, when she came home to find her grandfather lying on the floor of the kitchen.

'Grandpa!' cried Odile. She threw off the coat and ran to him. 'What happened? How long have you been lying there?'

'Nothing, nothing,' said her grandfather; but he let her help him up off the ground and into bed. 'I'm just a little chesty. It will pass.'

Doctors are not the best patients in any circumstances, but it is especially the case when they are simultaneously their own doctor and their own patient. It was two days before her grandfather admitted he needed help.

'There's a moss I need, for a broth,' he said. His breath came in gasps, in thick gulps laden with phlegm. 'The *ceratodon purpureus*.'

Odile nodded. Her grandfather had showed her its dried version in his stores. 'Fire moss?'

'You know what it looks like?'

'Yellow tips, with a red base?'

'Yes.' Her grandfather looked down at his hands, up at the ceiling; anywhere but at Odile. 'And you know where it is?'

Odile did know. Fire moss grew high on the opposite side of the mountain, away from paths, where the trees grew in contortions

8

and the wind was vicious. Kraik country. Without another word, she pulled on her boots and coat and kissed her grandfather's cheek. He waved her away; his skin was colder than usual.

Odile walked as far as the paths would take her, clapping her hands together in front and behind her back to keep them warm; and then she climbed. It was more of a scramble, really, around the edge of the mountain, but there were places where the ground cut away and dropped to a blur below. She did not fly: the wind might drop at any moment, and she didn't like the idea of so much gravity at once.

The first hint that something was wrong was the smell. Odile sniffed. There were seven layers of scent, none of them good: a between-the-toe smell, a week-old-fish smell, an unbrushed-tooth smell; a jackdaw's breath, a cat's sick pool, a burnt furball and a sailor's earwax.

'Kraiks,' she whispered.

She looked up, up the edge of the mountainside. She could see nothing – only mist, and branches stretching like arms across the rocks. But a voice came down, thin and quiet.

'Where are you going, little girl?'

Odile said nothing. She set her jaw, and kept climbing, heading sideways. There was a ridge in the mountainside, three feet wide, and she went slowly, keeping one hand on the rock.

'This is not your place,' said the voice. The Kraik spoke softly, as if it was merely telling the time.

Odile looked up despite herself. There was a clattering of wings, and a Kraik flew down out of the mist and perched on a rock above her head.

She had never seen one up so close. The Kraik had a long beak, a yellow head, a grey body and grey eyes. It stared at her. 'Did you

know that your face looks like the afterthought of a somewhat incompetent god?' it asked.

Odile tried to smile. She kept climbing. The trees creaked, beckoning, in the wind.

'Not far,' she whispered to herself. The moss grew on the inside lip of a cave, just twenty feet up and close to the mountain's peak. The mouth of the cave looked out onto a sheer drop.

Another Kraik flew down, and landed on a tree above her head. It had the face of an irate ballet mistress.

'Don't listen to him,' it said. 'Come up; see, that path, between those trees? Come up. We have what you're looking for.'

'You don't know what I'm looking for,' said Odile.

'Oh, but we do. We listen. We know more than you think. Look, and you'll see.'

The wind was beginning to blow the mist away. Odile looked up the side of the mountain.

Three Kraiks sat, waiting, at the mouth of the cave. As she watched, another one joined them.

One of them, who looked younger than the rest, shouted, 'You're even less pretty than you think you are. You have the face of a discontented horse.'

'You're a bird,' shouted Odile. 'And you smell like a hard-boiled badger fart.'

She climbed, faster, up towards where the birds congregated. The handholds in the rock grew farther apart, and the drop steeper. She tried not to look down. Panting, her mouth full of the taste of metal and fear, she reached the mouth of the cave.

She stood, sweat-smeared, waiting, staring at the birds. Nothing happened.

'The moss is right there,' rasped the Kraik, indicating the cave with its beak. 'Go in.'

Odile hesitated. The wind lifted her hair and blew it into her eyes.

'Are you a coward?' asked the bird. It gave a caw of laughter. 'Don't trouble to answer. It's written in your skin. Your hands are shaking.'

Odile bent her head and stepped into the cave. It was a small grey space, black in the shadow, with snow on the ground. The walls were lined with red and yellow moss.

The moment Odile was inside the Kraiks attacked. They descended on her in a cloud, beating their wings in her face, cawing out insults and war cries and shrill, meaningless shrieks.

'You're not as brave as you wish you were.'

'Every lie you've ever told will be discovered.'

Odile hit out, backing into the cave, but their talons clawed at her face and arms. 'What do you know?' she said. 'You're just birds.'

Odile crouched. Her arms were growing weaker; she grabbed a stick and swung it at them, but exhaustion was beginning to pull at her limbs. She sheltered her head with her hands, and tried to keep their talons out of her eyes.

The female Kraik landed on her knee. It pushed its beak into Odile's ear. 'Your grandfather never wanted you,' it croaked.

Odile's heart clenched. She looked up at the Kraik. The bird stretched its beak, in something akin to a smile. It looked confident; it looked certain.

'It would be a favour to him to give up now,' it said. 'You exhaust him. You're greedy and hungry and you break things and expect him to fix them. He loved your father, but you're nothing like him. Stop fighting. Do him a kindness.'

Odile pulled back her head and spat. Rage filled her arms and legs and she scrambled to her feet, pushing the bird onto its back and shoving the moss deep into her pocket. She backed to the edge of the cave, hitting out with both fists at the blur of feathers and claws, closed her eyes and dropped, backwards, off the edge of the mountain.

The wind roared. It lifted her. Out across a thousand feet of nothing Odile flew, the wind shaking her whole body, her outspread arms screaming with pain, flying faster than she ever had before.

She thumped down at the foot of the house and burst into the kitchen, her heart still tight with rage.

'There's your moss!' She slammed it down on the table. A mug rolled off the table and smashed. The old man looked up, startled, from his place in the armchair.

'Odile! What are you—'

Odile felt tears push against the backs of her eyes. 'They told me the truth. They told me you don't love me.'

'Odile—'

'They said I exhaust you.'

'Oh, my child.' The old man rose, rickety-legged and stern-faced. He took her face in his veiny hands. 'I told you not to listen to Kraiks.'

'But you said they knew—'

'They know fear, not truth. There's a difference.' With slow hands, he brushed the snow from her hair. 'I have loved you since the day you were born and I will love you until the day I die.'

'But they said—'

'No! There are no ifs or buts. Not with this kind of love.'

Odile felt her knees give way. She dropped down, and he caught her and pulled her onto the chair beside him. 'I thought,' she whispered, 'if you don't love me, that would mean I have nobody. If you don't love me, I'd be completely alone.' A white-hot wave rose up her chest and her voice halted, but she went on. 'I'm too afraid to be alone.'

'I know. I know.' Odile's grandfather nodded, and his neck creaked with the force of it. 'But there's no truth in that fear. When I die – which I don't intend to do for many years yet – the only thing you need do is show people love. The way you did when you went to find my fire moss.'

'That was just foraging.'

'It was love. And you'll find there will always be people to love you in return. Haven't I told you? Fear tells lies: trees masquerading as monsters, Kraiks' nonsense.'

Odile blew her nose on her finger and thumb. Her grandfather raised his eyebrows and fished a handkerchief from his pocket.

He said: 'And the one thing you *should* be frightened of, you never were.'

'What?' She blew her nose.

'Flying! But it never occurred to you to be afraid. You never did have any idea how brave you are.' He looked down, his eyebrows more than usually ferocious. 'Your father was the same.'

The wind swirled around the house, shaking the thick stone window frames. Odile looked outside. The mist had cleared, and the sky was snow-blue.

'Come,' said her grandfather. 'It's a good day for flying. What do you say we make this moss broth, and then you give me a go on my old coat?'

'*Your* coat?'

'Of course, mine,' he said. He smiled at her, and the smile made him look suddenly young. 'How else do you think I knew about the Kraiks?'

Illustrations by Chris Riddell

14

Peeva Is a
Tone-Deaf Cat

Anna Woltz

I wish I'd been born without ears. But you'd really need something else to put your hair behind, wouldn't you? You could have, say, two hooks in the shape of elephants' heads where your ears should be. And you could tuck your hair behind the trunks.

I'm the only one still at the breakfast table. Mum's playing the piano in the living room, Dad's upstairs listening to opera and Bruno, Finn and Seb are rehearsing with their band in the cellar. The whole house is thumping away – *their* house, I think angrily. It feels like they all live here and I'm just a guest.

But that means I've been a guest for eleven years. I must be on the longest journey ever.

I'm pretending to read the newspaper, but really I'm mostly looking at the pictures. Until one particular story leaps out at me:

WOMAN (70) DISCOVERS SHE WAS SWITCHED AT BIRTH

My heart starts pounding along with Bruno's drum, and the blood rushes and whistles through my ears. Because I've finally realized what my problem is. I read the story three times and then I sit there until my tea's gone stone-cold and I have a plan.

My brothers clearly have no idea why I've suddenly appeared in the cellar to fetch the pram. And I don't have a clue why Mum wanted to keep the thing after Seb. But I'm glad it's still there. I drag it *boink-boink-boink* up the cellar stairs, as my brothers launch into their favourite song, 'Peeva Is a Tone-Deaf Cat', for the hundred-millionth time.

'Arghh!' Finn yells after me. 'Could you at least try to make that din in time with the music?'

'Are you kidding?' I hear Bruno say. 'You know she's got absolutely no sense of rhythm!'

I sigh. Their song was called 'Eva Is a Tone-Deaf Cat' at first, but Mum got mad at them for being mean. Once they changed the title, though, she couldn't really object.

The pram's covered with cobwebs; it looks like something out of a horror movie. I brush the dust off the hood, push it up and down a bit, the wheels squeaking away, and then I dash upstairs. I gave up playing with dolls ages ago, but I kept the very biggest one, the best one, the one that looks just like a real baby. Carefully, I take Rose-Marie out of her cot. All of her bedclothes have to come too, because it'll work best if people can't see her too well. With my arms full, I race downstairs.

'Mum,' I call to the living room, 'I'm going to play outside.'

The piano concert stops for a moment.

'Have fun, sweetheart!' My mum's voice always sounds like she's singing. 'You'll be back in time for your judo, won't you?'

'*Yeeees!*' I yell back, far too loud. Knowing them, my brothers' next hit will be 'Peeva the Tone-Deaf Cat Howls the House Down'.

Obviously I don't remember being born. My first memory is from when I was four. We were at a concert that Dad was conducting, and I started screaming. I can still remember all the furious faces. And why I was screaming too: the music hurt my entire body, especially the soft bits of flesh under my nails. The musicians were playing medieval music on extinct instruments, and all I could think was: why on earth had someone decided to bring those instruments back to life? It was horrible. Like *Jurassic Park*, but in a concert hall.

But anyway, back to my birth.

I know from the stories that I was born at the hospital on the other side of the main road. No more than a quarter of an hour's walk from our house. While I'm waiting at the traffic lights with the pram, I look at the big white building. There it is, full of sick people and people who are almost dead, but somewhere inside is a ward of people who are only just beginning. Dozens of new little humans with no teeth, no scars and no tattoos. It must be impossible to tell so many babies apart all the time. And if you put them back in the wrong crib by accident, then they can't exactly shout out 'Hey, what are you doing?', can they?

Actually, when you come to think about it, it's a miracle that so many children end up living with their real parents.

I push the pram into the gleaming white lobby, and then I stop. It smells like first-aid kits and a bit like swimming pools. I see people with flowers, children with cards they've drawn themselves and patients in pyjamas wheeling around drips on poles.

Everyone's going somewhere, except for the boy who's waiting by the escalators with a banner. When the security guard comes closer, the boy quickly folds up his banner. But as soon as the guard turns his back, I can read what it says: EMERGENCY. NEED TO BORROW YOUR BABY. 1.75 FOR AN HOUR.

I push the pram towards him.

'Why do you need a baby?' I ask.

'None of your business,' he snaps back. And then he points at Rose-Marie, who's half-hidden under the covers. 'Can I borrow yours?'

'Maybe. But only if you tell me why.'

He sighs. His cheeks are pale and he's smaller than me. There's a picture of Spider-Man on his jumper.

'I was supposed to be getting a little sister,' he says. 'But something went wrong. Yesterday Mum was pregnant. And now she's not.'

I swallow. 'So why do you want to borrow a baby?'

'I just do…' He sighs. 'If I put a baby on her bed, maybe she'll stop crying for a minute.'

A man in a wheelchair comes by. His left leg is sticking straight out and it's covered in brand-new plaster.

'I'm really sorry about your little sister,' I say quietly to the boy. 'But my baby isn't real…'

He frowns. And then, before I realize what he's up to, he grabs all of the covers at once and pulls them out of the pram.

19

Rose-Marie's plastic face gives him an ice-cold stare, and I feel chills down my neck.

Tossing the covers back into the pram, he picks up his banner again. He doesn't glance at me, not even for a second. I can see that his chin's trembling, but he doesn't cry.

'Um, I don't know your name...' I whisper. 'But I do have a plan.'

He keeps looking straight ahead, like a soldier. 'My name's Tommy,' he says, his back straight. 'And I don't like other people's plans. I only like my own plans.'

'But what I have is a double plan,' I say quietly. 'My plan can go on top of yours...'

There's a little girl on the escalator with a big purple balloon. As she waves at someone I can't see, she accidentally lets go. The balloon flies up into the huge white lobby.

'All right, then. Tell me!' Tommy sounds impatient.

'You need a baby,' I say, 'and I'm on my way to the baby ward. That's why I brought the pram, as a disguise. If we go together, we can try to spot a baby lying around by itself somewhere. Then we'll switch the baby and my doll, and we can use the pram to take the real baby to your mum!'

Now Tommy is watching the purple balloon too, as it floats through the hospital, high above our heads.

'That,' he says, 'is the best idea ever. Come on, let's go.'

In the lift to the ninth floor, Tommy stands right next to me. 'So why do you have to go to the baby ward?'

Without saying a word, I take out the story I tore from the newspaper this morning. WOMAN (70) DISCOVERS SHE WAS SWITCHED AT BIRTH.

Tommy reads the first couple of lines and frowns. 'It didn't happen here, though, did it? It says Chicago. That's in America…'

As we step out of the lift, I don't say anything. But then I stop walking.

'It's not about that woman,' I whisper. 'It's about me. *I* was switched as a baby. *Here.*'

'Really?' His eyes widen. 'How do you know that?'

'It explains everything,' I say seriously. 'My whole family prefers music to hamburgers. They never talk – they sing instead. They always walk in time, they love extinct instruments, and my brothers tease me with stupid songs. Oh yes, and they fooled me into thinking that Schwarzkopf's a famous composer. But it's actually a shampoo.'

'It sounds more like a composer,' says Tommy.

I sigh. 'Yeah, that's what I thought too.'

Together, we walk to the ward with pink and blue elephants dancing over the walls. We keep perfectly normal expressions on our faces and we don't say a word about switching babies. The doors of most of the rooms are open. I see a woman lying in bed with a newborn in her arms. In another room there's a man walking up and down with a crying baby.

'There are parents everywhere,' Tommy whispers. 'This is never going to work.'

And then we spot a room where everyone's asleep. The mother in the hospital bed, the baby beside her in a crib made of see-through plastic.

'This one,' I say.

As silently as mice, we slip into the room. There are newly unpacked baby clothes and cuddly toys and picture books all

21

over the place. Tommy picks Rose-Marie up out of her pram, covers and all, and then his arms are full – which means I have to pick up the real baby.

It's a boy, I think, because he's wearing a tiny blue hat. His little nose is still flat from being inside his mummy's tummy, and they clearly haven't given him a proper wash yet.

Gently, I reach out my hand. I don't really have any idea how to pick up such a little baby. Do you start with the head? And should I take his blanket too? Just as I'm trying to wriggle my fingers under his body, the little boy wakes up. He stares at me drowsily, with gleaming eyes, and then he starts wailing. High and thin, like a goat kid bleating.

My heart forgets to beat for a moment, but before the mother even has time to move, Tommy and I go tearing out of the room. Me with the pram, him with Rose-Marie and all her covers.

'Slow down, you two!' shouts a nurse, but we don't dare hang around the ward a second longer than necessary. We race on as fast as we can. And we don't stop until we get to the lift.

'You see?' Tommy has two angry patches of red on his pale cheeks. '*That's* why I don't like other people's plans.'

He puts Rose-Marie back in the pram without even looking to see where her head is. His shoulders are drooping and I know he's thinking about his mum again. Yesterday she still had a baby in her tummy. And today she doesn't.

'You know…' I clear my throat. 'I get that your mum's sad. But at least she's already got a baby. A child, I mean. You, I mean.'

Tommy frowns. 'So?'

'You wanted to put a baby on her bed, didn't you? So that she'd stop crying?'

He nods.

'Well, have you tried putting yourself on her bed?' I ask. 'I mean… You're always standing down there in the lobby with your banner. But while you're away, she doesn't have any children at all.'

He picks at his Spider-Man jumper for a while before answering.

'Will you come with me?' he asks. 'Then you can take a peek around the corner first. To check if she's covered in tears and snot. If she's still not using tissues, I'm going straight back to the lobby.'

I hesitate. What I really want to do is go back to the baby ward, to see if there's anyone who's been working there for eleven years. Someone who happened to be at work on 7th June, when I was born. Someone who remembers that in the room next to ours there was a really nice mum who sang badly out of tune and couldn't play any instruments at all, but who was great at judo and making up stories.

But I don't dare to go back to the baby ward. And Tommy has this pleading look on his face. I sigh. I've only ever seen Mum crying when my gran died, and that felt terrible. Like nothing nice would ever happen again in the whole wide world.

23

'OK, then,' I say. 'I'll do a quick snot check.'

Silently, I follow him with the pram. We come to a long corridor where all the doors are closed. Right at the end, he stops. I park Rose-Marie and open the door a crack. The woman in the bed has the exact same face as Tommy, but with long hair and red lips.

'No snot,' I whisper to Tommy.

He presses his lips together and goes into the room. Slowly at first, but then he looks up at his mum and starts running. She holds out her arms and he climbs up next to her on the bed.

'Tommy!' His mum presses her cheek against his and hugs the Spider-Man jumper to bits. 'Where on earth did you get to, love? I missed you…'

As I look at the two of them in the bed, I feel a little bit angry. Tommy doesn't have to wonder for a second if he was switched as a baby. His mum is absolutely, definitely his mum – I can see that just by looking at them. A photocopier couldn't have done a better job.

Then she notices me.

'Hey…' she says in a surprised voice.

Tommy shrugs. 'This is Eva. She just came to do a quick snot check. And she was switched as a baby.' He beckons me over. 'Tell us about that story in the paper!'

I take the article out of my pocket and go closer. Then I tell Tommy and his mum all about the woman who found out at the age of seventy that her parents weren't her parents at all.

Tommy's mum looks at me curiously, with her head at a bit of an angle.

'The way you tell a story…' she says quietly. 'You do it just like my piano teacher. And you move the same as her too.'

'Nuuh-uuhhh!' Tommy cries. 'Eva isn't the slightest bit musical. And she thinks that shampoo's a composer.'

But I'm not looking at Tommy any more. I'm staring at his mum.

'Really?' I ask. 'I move like her? Even though I can't play the piano at all?'

She smiles. 'You talk with your hands. She does that as well. And there's something about your faces. Something serious and cheerful at the same time. You know, if you really were switched as a baby, then I reckon Sarah, my piano teacher, must be your real mum.'

I don't say anything else. If I preferred music to hamburgers, then I'd be able to feel a really loud concert in my body right now, with a big crowd shouting and cheering. But I'm pleased to say I don't hear anything at all. I can just see Tommy lying happily next to his mum in the bed. And I know my mum might not make the best copies ever, but she's done a pretty good job. Because Sarah the piano teacher is my mum. And she's been my mum for eleven whole years.

Translated from the Dutch by Laura Watkinson

Illustrations by Adam Stower

The Girl with No Name

Aline Sax

*For Nelle, who doesn't yet
know that she's called Nelle.*

1

She stirs her spoon around her bowl. The cornflakes swirl in the milk. They've gone soggy, and she doesn't like soggy. She looks at her mum and dad, but they're busy with their own breakfasts and aren't paying any attention to her.

'Why did you call me Nelle?' she asks suddenly. It's a question that's been bothering her for a while, and she'd finally like to know the answer.

'Why?' Dad says, his knife hovering over his slice of toast.

'Yes. Why? Why did you decide to call me that when I was born?'

Mum and Dad look at each other. Mum's shoulders go up high. 'Because we thought it was a nice name.'

'Why?'

'Because… um, well, we thought it sounded nice,' Dad says.

'But what does it mean?'

Now Dad shrugs too.

'Nothing. We just thought it was nice.'

Nice? What kind of answer is that? Why doesn't her name *mean* anything? You don't choose a name, a name she'll have to have all her life – for ever – just because it *sounds nice*, do you?

'But why doesn't it mean anything? A name has to mean something, doesn't it? You can't just string a bunch of letters together and make a name!'

'But a name doesn't really have to mean something, does it?' Her mum's voice is quiet. And a little doubtful. As if she's wondering if they chose the wrong name.

'Yes!' cries Nelle. 'It does!'

Don't they get it? She wants a name that says something, a name that has a meaning. Every name has a meaning. She's spent plenty of time thinking about it. Snow White means something. Red Riding Hood means something. Cinderella means something. Sleeping Beauty means something. Even Mum and Dad have a meaning. So why did they choose such a stupid name for her, one that doesn't mean anything at all?

27

'But, sweetheart,' Dad says, trying to calm her down. 'It doesn't really matter that much, does it?'

'Yes! It *does* matter!' Nelle bangs her spoon on the table. Drops of milk fly all around. 'I want another name. A name that means something!'

'Well, you can't just go and get another one, can you? You already have one.'

'I don't have a name. Not a *proper* one.' She crosses her arms and glares at them. 'And if you won't give me a proper name, I'll just go and find one for myself.'

'But, Nelle…' says Dad.

'No. I'm not Nelle. I'm a Girl with No Name! Until I find a proper one.'

Nelle pushes back her chair and leaves the kitchen.

In her room, she picks up her rucksack. She puts an apple in it, then a chocolate bar from the secret box under her bed and a warm jumper. She doesn't know how long it's going to take her to find a new name.

When she comes back downstairs, Mum and Dad are still sitting at the table, looking a bit stunned.

She slips past them and quietly closes the front door behind her.

2

The village is deserted. It's early. Everyone's probably still having breakfast. Nelle hooks her thumbs under the straps of her rucksack and starts walking quickly.

She follows the road that winds its way into the fields. Everyone in the village knows her already. She'll never find a new name there. The morning sun is stubbornly trying to break through the mist trailing over the meadows. Where should she begin? Who can help her to find a new name? The cows, up to their knees in the dewy grass, barely look up as she goes by. Maybe she should head into town. Lots and lots of people live there, with lots and lots of different names. It's a long way, but she has an apple and a chocolate bar with her, so she'll manage.

When she's walked a few hundred metres, she notices splashing sounds coming from a pond.

Down among the reeds, there's a boy crouching on a flat stone. He's skimming pebbles over the water. They skip across the surface like little frogs. Nelle pushes her way through the reeds and squats down beside him.

'What are you doing?'

The boy doesn't look up. He narrows his eyes to slits and throws another stone. It bounces twice before sinking into the water with a splash.

'Don't you have to go to school?'

'I don't want to go to school,' he replies. 'Everyone just laughs at me.' He tosses another pebble. It goes so far that it almost hits the duck bobbing around in the middle of the pond. The duck doesn't notice.

'What's your name?'

'Leon,' he says, without looking at her. 'How about you?'

'I don't have a name.'

Now he does look at her. Just a glance. Then he picks another stone out of the mud.

'Does that mean something? "Leon"?'

He throws the stone and counts how many times it bounces. Three times.

'My mum says it means "as brave as a lion".'

Brave as a lion! *Now that's what I call a name*, thinks Nelle. *Maybe I'd like to be called Leon too.*

'But it's rubbish.'

'Rubbish? Why?'

The boy shrugs.

'I'm not brave. If I was brave, I'd be at school. And I'd kick Billy's shins really, really hard. And I'd tell him what an idiot he is. And I'd tell him that my shoes aren't girls' shoes and that he can get lost. Him *and* his stupid mates.'

Nelle looks at his shoes, but they're covered in mud.

'Hmm, so your name's not right for you?'

Leon sniffs and throws a stone into the water so hard that it doesn't bounce at all, but just sinks with a big splash.

He won't be able to help her, then.

Nelle sighs.

3

As she walks on, Nelle tries to work out if it's worse to have no name at all or a name that's not right for you. But Leon does at least have an answer if someone asks him what his name means. And maybe he'll be brave when he grows up, and then his name will be right. After all, a name's something you have all your life.

A bell rings, startling her. The postman has to brake really hard to stop his bike, and he scrapes his heels on the ground. Clouds of dust billow up, making Nelle cough.

'Hey, daydreamer! Watch where you're walking!' laughs the man. 'Where are you off to? Shall I take you home?'

Nelle shakes her head.

'I can't go home yet. I'm looking for a new name.'

'A new name?'

'What's *your* name?'

'Everyone calls me Tubby.'

'Tubby?'

The postman smiles and pats his big belly.

'That's how I got it. People think all I ever eat is cakes.'

'Do you eat lots of cakes?'

'No, not at all. But I'm still Tubby. No matter how much I cycle.' He chuckles.

'So your name just says what you look like. Not what you're *really* like?'

The postman gives a shrug. 'It's the first thing people notice. They give you a name before they know you. I know plenty of names without actually knowing the real people behind them.' He nods at the large bags on the back of his bike. 'All those letters have names. I know exactly where the names live, what their houses look like and who their neighbours are. But I only know what a few of the people attached to those names are actually like. I have to get going now. Or I'll never finish my round in time.'

And, with a loud ring of his bell, the postman says goodbye.

Do I have to choose a name that describes what I look like? Nelle wonders as the cloud of dust left behind by the postman begins to settle. Then everyone will know who people mean when they talk about her. But she's not fat. And she's not really thin either. She not very tall and she's not very small. Her hair isn't a special colour, she doesn't have freckles and she doesn't have a limp. *Maybe I'd rather have a name that says more about me*, she decides, and she carries on towards the town.

4

The first building she comes to is a big farmhouse. Its red roof stands out against the grey of the surrounding sheds and stables. The gate that's supposed to close off the driveway to the farm is open and hanging at a crooked angle. Deep furrows in the ground lead to the barn and the field beside the house, where the corn is high. A dog comes running up. It barks at her, but it's just saying hello. Nelle braces herself as the dog comes to a stop just in front of her and pushes its big head against her leg.

'Lobo! Stop!' comes a voice from the house. Nelle ruffles the dog's black fur. In return, she feels a wet tongue on her hand.

'Lobo!' A man comes out of the house.

'Oh, I'm sorry. He's sometimes a bit too bouncy,' he says, pulling the dog away.

'I'm not scared of dogs.'

'Are you scared of pigs?' asks the farmer. 'Because mine are waiting to be fed.' He pushes a wheelbarrow full of big sacks towards one of the sheds. Lobo and Nelle follow him.

It's pretty dark inside. The big space is filled with a horrible smell and loud grunting and snorting. When her eyes have got used to the lack of light, Nelle sees a wooden fence in front of her. She stands on the bottom bar so that she can look over. There must be a hundred pigs in there, packed in together and wriggling away. A pink tangle of fat bodies, all bumping into one another and grunting as they root around in the mud. Lobo puts his nose between the bars of the fence and gives a big sniff. When the pigs hear the feed falling into their troughs, their grunts become even louder. They all want to be the first to reach the troughs. With their heads and their hindquarters, they try to push the others out of the way.

When all the sacks are empty, the farmer comes and stands beside her. Together, they watch the pigs gobbling down their food.

'There are so many of them. And they all look the same. How do you remember all of their names?' Nelle asks curiously.

'Their names?' The farmer raises his eyebrows. 'They're pigs. They don't have names.'

'Why not?'

'Why would I give them names? They're just pigs. They root around and they eat, and when they're fat enough they go to the slaughterhouse. They don't mean anything to me. Why would I give the creatures names? They're all interchangeable. One pig's much the same as another.'

'But the dog's got a name, hasn't he?'

'That's right,' says the farmer, scratching Lobo behind the ear. 'But Lobo isn't a pig. Lobo's my friend. We run the farm together. You only give names to those you love. Those pigs...' The farmer shrugs. 'I've got to get back to work now,' he says, leaving the shed. He whistles and Lobo runs after him. Nelle looks at the pigs again. She feels sorry for them, not having any names. That one with the black spot on his bum – she'd call him Spotty. And that one with the white tail... He'd be Whitetail. And that one has one sticking-up ear... But so does another pig over there. There are too many of them. And they all look too much like one another. After just three pigs, Nelle can no longer tell them apart.

As she walks back to the track, she thinks about what the farmer said. *Why would I give them names? They're all interchangeable.* She doesn't have a name any more either. Does that mean she's much the same as any other girl? It seems chillier now. As if the

34

mist has seeped into her body. She walks faster. She needs to find a new name as quickly as possible.

5

Nelle follows the track for what must be an hour without meeting anyone. The farmer's words are still with her, like a cold lump in her stomach. She has to find a name! But what if she can't? Will she always be the Girl with No Name? The girl no one cares about? But nobody comes along who might be able to help her. She's already finished her chocolate. She's getting tired, but she doesn't want to rest. Not until she's in town and has found someone who can help. After a while, she eats her apple too.

The sandy track turns into a tarmacked road. The grass on the verge becomes a footpath. More and more houses line the road. The first person she meets is an old woman. She's staring down at the ground, a shopping bag in her hand. A loaf of bread and a packet of biscuits lie at her feet. There's a carton of milk that's slowly emptying and a box of broken eggs that's popped open. Bits of a broken bottle of lemonade. Two bashed tomatoes and a red cabbage that have survived the fall. Three tins and an apple on the ground nearby. The woman's shoulders hang miserably and the corners of her mouth are trembling.

'Would you like me to help you?' Nelle picks up the tins and the apple. She gathers the bread and the biscuits in her arms. It's too late to rescue the eggs, the lemonade and the milk. The cabbage and the tomatoes balance on top of the other groceries.

'Thank you,' the old woman says. 'Would you walk back home with me?' Nelle nods. She doesn't ask where the old woman lives. But when, half an hour later, they still haven't arrived, she starts to become impatient. The old woman is stumbling along so slowly that it could take all day to reach her house. And Nelle still hasn't found a name. But she doesn't say anything and just follows the old woman, her arms full of groceries. Then, just as Nelle is starting to think that all the muscles in her arms are about to give way, the woman finally points at a little house at the end of a narrow street. She fiddles with her key in the keyhole and then leads Nelle down a dark hallway to a small kitchen. With a sigh of relief, Nelle lets the groceries slide onto the table.

Without saying anything, the woman makes two cups of tea and puts some biscuits on a plate.

'What's your name?' asks Nelle as she munches on a biscuit.

The woman has to think about it, as if it's a difficult question.

'I've had so many names,' she says with a faraway look in her eyes. 'Anna. Miss. Darling. Mum. Gran.' Her voice is soft, like she's just talking to herself. 'But these days no one really calls me anything at all.' She sighs. Nelle takes another biscuit.

'What's your name?'

'I don't have one.'

The woman raises her eyebrows.

'No one ever gave you a name?'

Nelle shrugs slowly. 'Well... yes, they did,' she admits. 'It's Nelle.'

'Nelle? It suits you,' says the old woman, thoughtfully.

'It suits me?' Nelle puts down her biscuit. 'But it doesn't mean anything at all! It just *sounds nice*!'

'You're wrong,' the woman replies. '*Nelle*. That's you. It's you and your helpfulness. Your patience. Your curiosity. I could see very well that I was walking too slowly for you and that there was somewhere you'd rather be. But you stayed and you helped me. And that was all you. Even with that frown on your face.'

'But…' Nelle's not sure she's really understood. 'Nelle doesn't mean anything at all, so how can it suit me?'

'Your name doesn't give meaning to you. It's you who gives meaning to your name.' The woman smiles and places her hand on Nelle's.

Nelle, thinks Nelle. *That's me. It means me.*

And she puts the whole biscuit in her mouth, all at once.

Translated from the Dutch by Laura Watkinson

Illustrations by Ross Collins

37

Mr Nobody

Laura Dockrill

1

'BOO!' he'd say. 'Be a dandelion for the day, spread yourself thin like jam, but not the pippy one, wink this eye and then the next, pretend your eye is a camera, make a memory, *snap snap snap*, you don't have to be afraid.' He growls in the amber glow of my room. 'If a monster comes out from underneath the bed I'll tell you what I'll do: I'll eat them up before they even think of getting close to you, you do know why, don't you? Because you're my priority in the whole entire world for ever and again.'

Then he would tickle my ribs until they fell apart like keys on a piano, *clunk. Plink. Plonk.* And the chords of my heart would smash out some awful tune of deep belly laughter, which was far too wild and sad for bed.

'Rest your head,' he would comfort me. 'You're being way too mischievous for bedtime – I don't know what's got into you.' He winked. And then he would take to his usual way of messing my room up nicely, the way he always did. Before stealing himself away into the wardrobe with a *shhhhh* and a gentle tiptoeing and knocking-overing of my life. '*See you in the morning,*' he'd whisper. '*Be there or be… a triangle.*'

And I could sleep. Just like that. In the safety of knowing he *was* there. Dozing. Looking out for me.

His name: Mr Nobody. But he was everybody, at heart.

You see, Mr Nobody is not a nobody of any kind. It's actually quite a humble and misleading name for such an explosion of a character. He wears a pecan-coloured suit and smart shiny shoes and a moustache and round glasses in perfect circles. His hat is round too, and his eyes are kind, and his briefcase swings to this side, and that and his heels *click clack* when he walks, but only I hear the song they make. Some days he carries an umbrella, even if it isn't raining, just to poke about and prod at stuff lined up on shelves and be intrusive and curious and bossy. And when he sneezes he sounds like a trumpet, and a small envelope of a hanky rolls out from his sleeve to collect the ideas that have snotted out of his dreaming head with a *BANG!*

2

'WHAT DO YOU WANT TO DO TODAY?' he shouts, spitting golden dots of cornflakes in my face; he never closes his mouth when he chews, he wears odd socks and crooked shoes, his eyes scream love and chaos and when Mum isn't looking he tips jelly beans into my cereal bowl and spoons them down to hide in the milk. Our dog, Roly Poly, doesn't like him when he's naughty, and he tries to be a singing canary and tell on Mr Nobody to Mum, but Roly only speaks dog language so Ha. Ha. Ha.

I say, ' I don't mind. What do *you* want to do, Mr Nobody?' And he replies with a smirk that I know is dangerous. A smile that means adventure.

We run to the station, the wind flapping our coats, and Mr Nobody has to hold on to his hat with one hand, but he laughs at the wind, and the cats in windows glare at us all aggressive with seething jealousy. He jumps the barriers and I shout *you can't do that*, and he says *who says?*

You can't charge money for being free.

We eat red sweets on the train and people smile at us. We go upside down and let our feet be on the ceiling and we play a word game, and then Mr Nobody brings out his harmonica and cries out some dreadful tinny noise that convinces me that he has zero musical talent, but he is talented in many other ways, so it's fine. You can't have everything. He says *perhaps one day, you'll be like me*. And I say *I hope not* but really I mean *I hope so*.

We eat chips and curl down the streets and bump and barge and cause havoc. We laugh at pointless things and take the time to make the limpest of meaningless things seem meaningful, treat the tired like treasure. In the bookshop, Mr Nobody rips out the back pages and swaps them with the back pages of other books, *it makes the ending more exciting* he sniggers, and I pretend I'm cool with it but secretly do coughing every time he rips a page to protect us. I'm a medium-to-extra-large goody-goody if I'm brutally honest.

At the beach we throw stones into crashing waves and forget our ages. The sea is the most victorious queen beast that ever lived, but Mr Nobody runs in fully clothed. Although respectful to Her Majesty, he is not scared of anything. Fearless. He's left slicked by salt, and tar-black with wetness. He shivers. Otter-like. His lips blue. His teeth chatter. I call him *silly*.

He pats his hands like he's wearing oven gloves and gets all serious, *you're getting older, Oliver, one day you might not wonder or care about me any more.*

I say that that's impossible.

And lead him to the café toilets, where they are bound to have one of those hand-drier things to dry him off with.

3

'Stop talking about Mr Nobody,' my big brother Luke says. He is playing a computer game, his imagination is tanked, his patience lost. 'At secondary school they'll make fun of you.'

'No they won't!' I argue back. 'And even if they do, Mr Nobody will absolutely annihilate them.'

'That's not how it works, Oli,' he mutters. 'It will be *me* having to annihilate them. That's who.'

Mr Nobody doesn't like fighting, so Luke might be right.

'What am I supposed to do then: ignore him?'

'Yeah. Maybe.' Luke loses a life and grunts like it's my fault. 'Just at school in between the hours of eight and four.'

'That's too long!' I panic. 'He'll crinkle up and die of dried-up boredom.'

'No he won't. Can't you just leave him here at home with some snacks and a film?'

'No! I can't just leave him here – he comes everywhere with me, Luke.'

'Well… maybe it's time he stopped?'

My heart: a stone rock. My throat: a glass of mud.

'You sound like Mum.' I try not to cry. I hold the tears back like the way the roaring sea wants to touch my cold feet when it can't. 'Mr Nobody says HI by the way! Just because YOU forgot about him doesn't mean he forgot about YOU!' I roar and slam my door and hear the hanger with my new school blazer hurdle towards the ground.

I do not pick it up.

Luke is right. Mr Nobody can't come to secondary school. He wasn't even welcome at my *babyish before* school, where the world tumbles on simply round, bowed like a rainbow and endless, and everything is welcome. And uncomplicated. And everybody wins. And every direction is a yes.

Even then, he was a sore thumb. He got me into trouble. He made me seem a fool.

4

'Oh, what am I like? I've walked into another lamp-post,' Mr Nobody jokes, miming a sore head. 'You can't take me anywhere!' He tuts, grinning, he swirls his head like he's seeing cartoon stars. He's trying to cheer me up. But he's right. I *can't* take him anywhere. Not in real life.

'I know...' he tries. 'What's black and yellow and explosive?'
'I dunno.'
'A BOMB-le-bee!' he presents, proudly.
'I've heard that one before.'

Mr Nobody's face falls off. He looks all blurred in, like the moon. I feel a stab in my gut.

'Want to play hide-and-seek?' he suggests, hopeful.
'No. I want to lie here and think.'
'THINK?' Mr Nobody splutters. 'Since when did you think?'
'It's an actual thing to do, OK? You're meant to do thinking when you're more older, we don't all just *act* the way YOU do.'

Mr Nobody's feelings are maybe a bit hurt.

'OK. Well… then… I guess I'll just…' He walks away, but a flame of enthusiasm lets him have one more go: 'Are you sure you don't want to cut up a watermelon and eat it by the—'

'Yes. I am sure,' I say, all harsh. The words cut bullet holes into my teeth.

And Mr Nobody takes his hat off, scuffed soles heading heavily out of my bedroom. 'Mr Nobody?'

'Yes, Oliver?' He looks up, his bug eyes wet.

'Close the door behind you.'

And he is gone.

5

I think I see Mr Nobody's head pop out behind some bushes. Everybody seems to look like him. I smell his musty dusty warm smell floating through the air like summer. His voice crackles in my eardrums like an old record turning round. Stupid big ugly school. I don't want to go.

The orange crisp leaves are battered cods, my uniform is too big, my bag too heavy. The journey to school too different. And Luke walks ahead with his friends with long legs and big shoulders and voices that curve unbalanced in and out of old and small.

I think I see Mr Nobody's face smile at me through the gates. He is right. I am getting older.

I am growing up.

And I don't think I like it one bit.

6

Our first day gets to be still quite babyish, which obviously I am secretly grateful for. We get to label up our books and play these annoying name games and I think our teacher is actually OK. Then we get given paper and pens, even coloured felt-tips, which I thought were extinct and illegal at this stage in our lives, but clearly not. We are asked to write about ourselves and title it: About Me. We can illustrate the pieces and even lay them out however we actually want.

I write my name out in bold letters: OLIVER.

And my age: 11.

I draw Mum and Luke and Roly Poly.

I draw my house.

And the TV.

I write that I like trains. And music. And space is OK. My favourite food is pizza. It feels weird to not write about Mr

Nobody, because he is the main thing I think makes me me. The page feels empty without his name on it. If I see him again, I won't tell him that I left him off. I feel guilty about that.

Some of the new people in class don't mind *sharing* theirs. But I mind. And say nothing. And even though my hand didn't go up, my heart still beats so loud in my chest.

The teacher asks if we could all bring in a photograph of ourselves tomorrow; she says, *choose a photo from when you were young to illustrate the words*. She says *it might be best to bring a copy of the photo in case it's precious*.

I think of the photo of me with the sandcastle.
  Or when me and Luke jumped off the bridge into the lake.
  Or the one from my fifth birthday party: it was jungle-themed and I went as a leopard. I think I got food poisoning after that. And Mr Nobody slept on my bedroom floor that night curled up like a prawn.

I don't see Mr Nobody on the walk home.
  I don't see anybody.

7

Mum strokes my hair and says she is proud of me. She says she remembers when I was small and just only began nursery and now here I am, becoming a big boy. I say *don't call me a big boy*. It sounds oddly babyish, even though it's actually not at all.

She kisses me and says goodnight. She says I have another big day to look forward to tomorrow. I try to close my eyes before the click of the door, the swelling darkness.

Mr Nobody does not come to say goodnight. He does not make me laugh or mess up my room.

They say all you have to do is lie down. Lie down. And close your eyes. Lie down and close your eyes and breathe, normally. But then maybe also take deep breaths too. Just for relaxation. They say try not to think of anything, but maybe it also helps to think of things too, soft things that won't upset you or make you sad or anxious or worried or too excited, just nice things, slow things... penguins. Or sheep. Or clean washing, on the line, blowing in the wind.

I try to think of a tree, covered in white balloons. The balloons drifting off, one at a time into the clear-blue sky...

But it never works.

I always think of that one balloon, left behind, stuck in the branch of a tree until it shrinks and shrivels, limp with the birds. Alone.

I whisper...

'I miss you, Mr Nobody. I'm sorry I told you to go away.'

But he doesn't hear me, and even if he did, he doesn't let me know.

8

'Doesn't Mr Nobody like his cereal any more?' Mum asks in front of Luke. I shudder.

'No, he's gone,' I softly say. Luke feels bad, I think, and drinks his tea down in one hot gulp. I imagine the dots on his tongue burning off as he leaves the table.

Mum rolls her eyes and calls him *grumpy*. She shows me some photos to take in. There is one of me and Mr Nobody. But I won't be using that one.

'You don't have to call him Mr Nobody any more, I shouldn't have said that.' Mum kisses me; she smells of burnt toast and bed. 'I'm sorry, I didn't mean to confuse you or make it hard for you. We all miss him.'

9

The wall in our classroom is covered with our faces and words. There is Mabel who likes ice cream on the beach with her aunt. Zach who likes football and KFC. Ameet who has *quite bad asthma*. Mina who likes drawing fairies and has a pig nose, but she left that bit off.

I choose the photograph of me and Luke jumping off the bridge into the lake.

'Why don't you use this one?' my teacher suggests. 'You look so happy.'

She's pointing to the one of me and Mr Nobody.

I go quiet.

'I don't like it.'

'Aww, why not? Who is that?'

She points to his smiling face, while he's holding me, tickling my ribs until they fall out of my chest, squeezing me in, both of us laughing our heads off, his crushed eyes, like fortune cookies, cheeks red.

'It's Mr Nobody.' I reply.

'Mr Nobody? How mysterious,' my teacher answers kindly, 'but surely everybody is a somebody?'

'He is my granddad,' I say, 'but Mum got upset when he came to visit because he's all died now.'

'I'm sorry, Oliver. So you named him Mr Nobody to not upset your mum?'

I nod. 'It's not my fault he still wanted to say goodnight.'

'No it's not your fault at all – I think it's perfectly normal to want to say goodnight to somebody that you love.' She smiles warmly. 'My granddad died too.'

'So did my one too,' a girl with orange hair offers. 'You're not alone.'

I stick the photograph of me and Mr Nobody on my About Me sheet.

I draw an arrow telling the world exactly who he is.

Illustrations by Neal Layton

Pipounette's House

Ludovic Flamant

1 – The Dream

Pipounette was rather grumpy when she woke up that morning. Her old joints hurt, but worse than that, she hadn't been able to finish her dream. She'd been dreaming of a train coming out of an elephant's trunk – a white elephant at that! Not the kind you meet every day! The train rushed towards her, without rails, like a long crazy caterpillar, then slowed down as it saw her. The engine driver leant out the window. He was going to tell Pipounette something really important – she could tell from the particular way he gathered his lips. But just when he reached Pipounette and could finally utter the words, her alarm rang. The old woman was quite angry with herself: why had she set her alarm on a Saturday morning when there was nothing to prevent her lounging in bed till noon?

She went downstairs to the kitchen to make some pancakes to cheer herself up. Pancakes are generally a good way of cheering yourself up. Waffles, too. And chocolate. Pipounette sighed as she passed a mirror: *Just look at that fat behind! I'm having to cheer myself up a lot these days*. Winter was dragging itself out, it must be said, and the grey days were not helping her mood. *I think I'm better off returning to bed*. Which is what sent Pipounette back beneath her duvet, where she picked up her dream at the

exact point it had stopped: the engine-driver opened his mouth and said clearly: 'Your nephews have just arrived at the station, Miss Pipounette.' Pipounette leapt out of bed: 'My nephews! Of course, my nephews! I'm late!'

2 – The Reunion

Tamanoir and Tamandoua were waiting obediently at the station, in the lost-property office. They'd been placed atop a stack of suitcases and umbrellas. 'Aunt Pipounette!' they cried when they saw her arrive. She led both of them to the rear of the little trailer she always kept hooked to the back of her tandem. 'My! Haven't you got heavy, the pair of you! It was easier when Georges was here to pedal with me.'

'You want us to help you?'

'No, you're my guests and we're nearly there.'

Tamanoir and Tamandoua knew the ritual by heart: first they must choose a bedroom before night fell, for many of the rooms were not lit. They were already familiar with seventeen of the bedrooms. The question was always whether they wanted to find a room they'd liked the previous year or discover a new one. But the choice was made more difficult by the fact that although most of the rooms were for welcome guests, there were also a few rooms for unwelcome guests which were quite inhospitable, and this was not always immediately obvious.

That evening, they ate pancakes and attempted to get the music machine to work. This large clockwork orchestra had been built by Uncle Georges and was operated by four crank handles. But they were one person short, so the machine remained silent.

'Right, let's get to bed,' said Pipounette briskly. 'We'll start the explorations tomorrow.'

3 – The House

It was Uncle Georges who had built the entire house as a surprise for Pipounette. He had constructed it in secret for her and the many children they would one day have together. They were both very young at the time. One morning he silently placed a bunch of keys on the pillow beside her along with a note, which read: 'My darling, I have built a large castle with infinite rooms for us. Here is the address. Meet me there this evening after I finish work.' Georges worked in a factory that made holes, deep holes of earth. Pipounette shivered with pleasure at the idea of this house with infinite rooms. She hadn't had her morning kiss (he had let her sleep), but she would give him a thousand kisses that evening. That day there was an awful accident at Georges's factory and a hole collapsed on top of him. Georges never made it to their evening rendezvous in the large house. Pipounette waited and waited, her mouth brimming with kisses for him. They would never have children. That's life. But every year, when the swallows returned to nest beneath the roof of the veranda, she had her nephews over to explore the house. With their help she discovered rooms, nooks, corridors and spaces. Every year they asked: 'Auntie, what are we looking for?' and each time she answered: 'We'll see as we go.'

4 – The Departure

They filled their backpacks with flasks, food, rope, torches, walkie-talkies, string and pebbles, and set off. They also took paper and pencils so that, year by year, they could compile a more complete map of the house. The problem was that each time they were obliged to start from the same point, the kitchen, meaning they lost several hours going through the rooms they had previously explored before they could discover new ones.

'Why do you only live in the kitchen, Pipounette?'

'Oh you know, when you live alone you might think you have more space than when living with someone else, but it's the opposite: everything seems too big. So you carve out a little place that fits you, and you soon forget the rest exists.'

Pipounette often said odd things like that. For example, she also said: 'When you don't know what decision to take, just pick up any book, open it and point at a sentence at random. Sometimes you have to interpret a bit, but the sentence always tells you what to do. After all, if you don't know what to do yourself, better to let chance decide.' This last thought was most timely, since they had just happened upon an unknown room filled with sand, the walls of which were covered with around fifty doors, each of them different from the next.

5 – The Doors

'We must stay together, whatever happens.' Tamanoir and Tamandoua nodded. Tamanoir rummaged in his bag for a white pebble, which he placed on the ground: 'That way, when we return we'll know which door we used to get here.' Tamandoua added, 'Now we need to know which door to take. We would do well to stop a moment and ponder the matter. Pipounette, do you think there might be doors with traps?'

'Well, there are rooms for unwelcome guests, so why not? Perhaps this very room is a trap.'

'Yet everything seems fine: the floor isn't collapsing under our feet and no tiger has leapt out to attack us.'

'True, but we're really not sure. We daren't go any further.'

'Well, that means we need to pick the right way!'

'That's the trap, though. If I asked you to choose between a cherry pie and an apple pie, could you do so?'

'Yes, I prefer apples.'

'And if I asked you to choose between a glub pie and a zborg pie?'

'I don't know what they taste of…'

'Exactly. You can only choose between things you know, but we don't know what lies behind these doors. The only choice we can make when faced with the unknown is to simply go for it, or not.'

'So the trap is believing that you need to pick a door!'

'Exactly. You have to choose something, but not a door: you have to choose between staying here for ever or returning where you came from or… carrying on the journey.'

'Carry on!' cried Tamanoir and Tamandoua with one voice. They stepped through any old door and ended up any old place.

6 – Any Old Place

Any old place was the largest room they had yet found in the house. It was a huge library with ladders going up to little balconies. Large chandeliers sparkled from the ceiling like at the opera. Here and there were several deep leather armchairs with a plaid shawl draped over the back and, next to each one, a coffee table on which sat an empty cup, an assortment of tea bags and a plate of biscuits. In the centre of the room was an open fire, which had burst alight of its own accord as soon as they entered. A highly excited Tamanoir and Tamandoua rushed to climb the ladders: 'Oh look! Comics! Thousands of comics! And there, books of experiments and magic tricks!'

They explored all the shelves of comics, with cries of joy. Pipounette wandered the room at a calmer pace. All these treasures had lain dozing here for years without her knowing. For no one. Suddenly weary, she sat down in one of the armchairs. Out of habit, she reached for a biscuit, but it was much too old to still be edible. She threw it into the open fire. That's when she noticed the book lying on the table. Its handwritten title said: *Love Poems for Pipounette*. It was Georges's handwriting. She read the first poem then a second one and then another. She wept. They were all so beautiful. All of them promised Pipounette eternal love. 'We shall always be together,' they said.

Pipounette felt the disgust rise in her and she couldn't stop it: it was just a lie, Georges was dead. So she got up and threw the book into the fire.

7 – The Fog

As it burned, the book began to give off a huge quantity of smoke. A thick white smoke that soon poured out of the open fire and filled the entire room. 'Tamanoir? Where are you? Tamandoua? Can you hear me?' It was impossible to see anything at all, and the library was so vast that none of them could find their bearings. The walkie-talkie crackled from the depths of Pipounette's bag: 'Hello? Hello? Auntie Pipounette?'

'I hear you loud and clear, boys. Where are you?'

'We don't know, but we're leaning against a wall. Walk along the wall, and we're bound to meet at some point.' Pipounette walked straight ahead until she reached a wall, then followed it. But it was a wall with an opening, which meant she soon entered another room without realizing.

'Hello? Are you still there?'

'We're waiting for you,' said the voices in the walkie-talkie, growing fainter and fainter. The batteries were dying. She stopped, fumbled in her bag and found the torch. She turned it on, but couldn't see any better. *What's the point if there's nothing to see?* she thought. Pipounette removed the batteries from the torch to replace those in the walkie-talkie. It began to work very well again. 'You are nearly here, my love.'

'Pardon?'

The voice at the end of the device had changed. It was no longer Tamanoir's or Tamandoua's.

'Move away from the wall. Take three steps to your side and listen.'

Pipounette did so. She found that she had stepped into a draught that cleared away the smoke somewhat. Listening carefully, she could hear breathing.

'I'm here', said the voice in the walkie-talkie.

She walked carefully in that direction. There was less smoke now. A shape became visible, like a kind of large rock. But the rock moved and breathed in such a way that Pipounette eventually realized that it was in fact an elephant. A very large white elephant.

8 – The Elephant

She expected to see a train come out of it, like in her dream. But this was no exit elephant, it was an entry elephant.

'Come along,' said the voice in the walkie-talkie. 'It's this way.'

The elephant's trunk was as wide as a little tunnel, the kind you might crawl through in a playground.

'I'm too old for this,' complained Pipounette as she thrust her head into the trunk. Inside, everything was lit up with a bright, warm glow.

'It wasn't very nice of you to burn my poems. I wrote them for *you*.'

Georges was sitting there in a suit, smiling.

'It wasn't very nice of you to have left me all this time,' replied Pipounette.

She wanted to wrap her arms around him, but he wasn't very substantial; rather like a sort of ghost you can see very clearly but not quite touch.

'I suppose that my time has come and that death has sent you to fetch me?' asked Pipounette.

'Oh no, not at all!' Georges answered with an amused air. 'One day I left without saying goodbye. I never imagined what would happen then, of course. I have come to give you your morning kiss.'

He kissed her once on the forehead, once on the nose and once on the mouth.

They talked a little more, then sat there quietly, gazing into each other's eyes. Finally, Georges said:

'Tamanoir and Tamandoua will be waiting for you.'

'They can wait a little longer. But will we see each other again?'

'It all depends where the elephant wants to go.'

'Georges… I think I have loved you nearly every moment of our life.'

'Me too, Pipounette.'

9 – The Machine

She found Tamanoir and Tamandoua. They used the maps and the pebbles to find the kitchen again. And that evening they all gathered around the music machine: Tamanoir, Tamandoua, Pipounette and an old neighbour who rarely went out.

'Why did you fit the machine with four crank handles?' Pipounette had asked Georges in the elephant. 'Even with both of us, we could never have made it work.'

'It's a festive machine,' he had replied. 'I built it that way on purpose, to oblige us to invite friends round, and neighbours too, and get to know the people in our local area.'

And that's how the neighbour came to be there.

The four of them turned the crank handles at the same time. The machine came to life, and the music it produced was truly beautiful. It's never too late to listen to good music.

Translated from the French by Roland Glasser

Illustrations by Anna Höglund

The Roof

Nataly E. Savina

In the beginning, Grandpa and Grandma would sit with me on the beach every day, with a stopwatch, to get me used to the sun. One minute the first day, two the next, then they'd always wrap me up in a towel. I can't remember Grandma; I was just a baby at the time. But I do recall how Grandpa used to greet me the same way each year:

'You're as white as milk! We'll have to do something about that right away!'

We'll clear out the flat, then we won't be coming back for a while, says Mama. Her eyes shimmer like two lakes in the rain. It used to take us four days to get here by train; now it's just a few hours' flight. As soon as we've got our suitcase, Mama looks for a taxi. Her shoulders droop like the wings of a tired bird. We have another hour's drive through the dark, that's the way it's always been – except that Grandpa always used to pick us up in his Zhiguli. I stroke Mama's shoulder blade under the green summery silk and resolve to memorize everything. I must gather puzzle pieces for our memories, so as not to lose the last few years.

Gazing out of the taxi window with the warm wind blowing in my face, I remember how the wild cats used to do their business among the almond trees and only half-bury it, and how Fridays were always bath day at Grandpa's, so I'd have to go home earlier than all the other children.

When the car stops, there's a smell of petrol. Mama opens the heavy iron door, and I follow her inside to the foot of the stairs. The green letterboxes have rust patches now, but the dusty crack in the plaster still looks like a giant octopus. There's a smell of chicken soup and fried potatoes with garlic, but not from our door. Crockery clinks somewhere. Nothing has changed in Grandpa's flat. It's as if he's just popped over the road for a loaf of bread.

Olga heard our taxi arrive last night, so as soon as breakfast's over she's waiting with the others in the courtyard. She admires my mother, who never has a man with her and always wears such beautiful clothes. Like every year, we get together and form a small army – the children from the three buildings that are squeezed in like sardines between the outermost main road and the newly built-up area. Among the bramble bushes, we reach a decision:

we're going to make the caretaker's life a misery. We spit cherry stones and sunflower-seed husks onto the paths, wipe our muck-encrusted shoes on the broken benches in the yard. We sneak after him, lurking like little demons in every nook and cranny. Last year's dead cat – that's what the caretaker has to pay for. Even if he tells lies and claims it was us children who did it.

I'm the one who annoys him most: the skinny city child with the flaxen hair, my uppity mother's precious jewel. He loathes my pitying expression when I turn my head to look at him, just as we're about to make ourselves scarce after the latest prank. Pale and slow though I am, I have a hand in everything. I stumble and fall twice as often as the others. It's a miracle that I've never done myself a serious mischief. This summer I learn new swear words. Grandpa wouldn't have approved. I'll keep them for school; maybe I'll make a note of them. Then, in the showers after PE, when I'm the most suntanned of all, maybe I'll secretly pass them on to the others in my class.

Looking at the door frame where Grandpa used to mark my height each year, I can see I've grown a whole three centimetres. Mama is busy wrapping up his model ships in paper at the moment and can't help me, so I make the last mark on Grandpa's door, just above the crown of my head. I won't be growing any taller in this flat. The children's whistles echo outside, just as if they were in the next room. I drop the pencil and storm down the stairs and out of the building like a superhero, three steps at a time.

Last week a man with a rifle took a pot shot at the lads while they were out scrumping cherries. I'm sorry I wasn't with them. That tingling in your fingers and toes – it's a sign of life. Anyway, that old soak of a caretaker is an irritation. Some of the neighbours like us kids. But not a single grown-up around here has an ounce of respect for him. All of them laugh at him, the oddball. If he could, he'd fling his bottle at us. That's out of the question, of course. He has to secure everything that might harm us and keep tabs on it. It's his job to work for us, says Olga, making a nonchalant gesture like one of the musketeers from the TV series.

The girls envy Olga her older brothers, who are in the Navy and sometimes bring her things from overseas. To the boys, she's a queen. She has black eyes and black hair; they call her 'the Night'. Olga has read my palm, and now I know I'm going to live till I'm ninety. That means nothing can happen to me, I reassure my anxious mother in my thoughts – I'm going to live to be as old as old can be! But I already know I'll never be happier than I am this afternoon under the lorry tarp, where I and Olga set off a stink bomb. Who wants to be old anyway?

The caretaker must know we're just waiting for him to make a mistake. But leaving the door to the attic ajar is not an oversight. He's seen us sneaking around nearby. This is the only unexplored attic in the neighbourhood, after all. Olga, who lives in the same building, is in front of it now, smiling and beckoning. Together with the other lads I follow her call, up six flights of stairs, and then even farther, up the thin-runged rusty ladder.

There's nothing in the attic but junk, yet it's like a mousetrap. Like a hole full of honey into which the caretaker has lured us, the vermin. Most likely, he's often pictured himself towering above us and our cheeky faces, teaching us to show him some respect. How exactly he's going to do that he's not yet sure: by bawling at us, maybe, or by staying silent as the grave and breathing heavily, his fists clenched. All the caretaker knows is that it's dark and cold up there, with no parents around. And no maze-like streets, either, that would allow us to spread out like a swarm of cockroaches. The caretaker stomps up the stairs in pursuit, making plenty of noise to scare us. He's got us cornered. He watched Olga gathering us all around her and laughing at him, the dimwitted caretaker, for forgetting to lock the door. He watched us docile little sheep following the precocious siren in through the entrance. He knew we'd haul ourselves up the creaking ladder one after the other, into the attic, into the trap.

A panicky whispered warning spreads though our group when we hear the footsteps. Olga, the last on the way up, leaps lightly off the ladder and disappears like a fleeing nymph through the door to her parents' flat. Left behind, the boys and I have no chance. Faster than anyone can think a clear thought, we clamber out of the little slanted skylight onto the roof. I hear the crotch of my jeans tearing as I raise my leg. I'd trimmed them to have cut-offs for the summer. Olga has the same. In all the excitement, no one notices the rip. I glance behind me. Climbing the ladder, the caretaker tries to put on an authoritarian expression. But like someone in the middle of doing a sum who suddenly realizes he's losing his grip on the figures through sheer concentration, his features are now lost in a thicket of confusion. Swiftly, we all clamber as far up the roof as we can and crouch behind the chimney.

The caretaker thinks the attic is empty – but only for an instant. The kids have climbed onto the roof, he now sees. The skylight is open, and each of the caretaker's steps sounds as if he's dragging iron feet over a magnetic floor. What if one of us has fallen to the ground? Already? And if someone panics – what then?

Eyeing the black slates, I think how slippery they look. The sun has heated the tiles and the air is shimmering above them. My freckly shoulders are turning pink. My gaze wanders over the railing that runs along the edge of the roof. It's supposed to stop lumps of ice falling off the roof. As if it ever snowed here. What it really looks like is a parapet for dolls. It wouldn't hold my weight – it's too fragile. Olga's Barbie could lay her hand on it if she were standing on a dolls' bridge, gazing romantically into the glittering blue in the distance, but under my weight it would bend down towards the market in the street. Towards the tiny wrinkled market grannies with their vegetables, tiny brightly coloured dots with their headscarves and wraparound dresses. I like the idea. I feel light. It's an ideal opportunity to see if I can fly.

The caretaker knows I'm on the roof as well. And he knows full well who my mother is too; there's enough gossip about her in the neighbourhood. She'd put a death-dealing spell on him if anything happened to me. He sticks his head out of the skylight, as if under a guillotine, and his gaze turns automatically to the chimney. We're crouching there, our coltish legs bent. Four children, four small faces.

'Wetting yourselves now, aren't you?' he calls out, startled by his own steady voice.

He croaks out a forced smile, his panic-stricken eyes searching our faces for any expression.

'Come down from there right now!' His voice is hoarse.

Absently, I watch the lads crawl down slowly one after the other, guilt in their faces. It doesn't look that hard. One of them, Stas,

caught an infection from a stray cat and has been shaven-headed ever since. Olga told me his hair will never grow back.

Stas's ears are strawberry-red. But the caretaker's face is as white as if someone had shoved his head into a pail of flour. If I have to climb down the same way, I think, they're all going to notice the rip in my jeans, and they'll see what's underneath.

The skeleton pops into my head. It was last year, when I was at the market with Grandpa. He was arguing with one of the market women about the price of her eggs, and I felt embarrassed for him and fixed my gaze on a medical magazine lying next to the basket of eggs on the table. There was the skeleton, against a black background, grinning me in the face with every bone in its body.

Suddenly it comes to me that it was around the same time I heard the caterwauling from the basement. The caretaker must have heard it, just as I did, for several nights in a row. He could have gone down and let the cat out. The caretaker's eyes look as though he too has been forcibly reminded of this. The boys' brown legs come down towards him, one boy after another. The caretaker is obliged to hold the small bodies. He counts them. Their bellies are hot and sweaty; it's a sweltering day, even more so on the roof than anywhere else.

I'm the only one still on the roof. The caretakers shoos the scared boys out of the attic. But I stay put, motionless. None of his calls of encouragement have got through to me. Wearily, he fetches a crate, climbs onto it and pushes his way out of the window like a flower on a bent stalk. He too must be able to hear the swishing of the treetops now. He moves very cautiously, as though trying to catch a sparrow.

I stare at the rounded crowns of the trees, whose leaves brush the building with each gust of wind. The swishing hypnotizes me. I think of my school, the puddles covered with ice in the playground and the sleet that sometimes lashes me and Mama on our way through the city when she fetches me in the afternoon.

If I slip off the roof now and fall, it'll be straight into the rustling, velvety armchair of leaves. Underneath, branches await me which are normally beyond my reach.

I've only climbed really high once – when I was picking cherries for Grandpa last year. No one else saw me. No one but Grandpa. Afterwards we sat together in the kitchen at the enamel tub, and I watched Grandpa picking the stones out with Grandma's hairpin, preparing to make jam on the gas stove. The cherry juice ran over his hand and down his fingers, and sploshed into the tub, heavy as blood.

I feel the pull. It's the same visceral feeling you get in a moving lift, a pleasurable rushing sensation. More than anything, I want to leap up, spread my arms out wide and utter a long, high-pitched shriek, like a bird. My body is electrifying alive, and I think, 'Till I'm ninety!'

With ice-cold fingertips I sit there, looking down on the trees and the tiny, bustling human ants. I'm leaning against the chimney, but not holding on to it. The blood throbs in the caretaker's large ears, but I can't hear it. My face begins to look relaxed and happy; no one but Grandpa has ever seen me like this. The caretaker climbs a little farther out of the window, but I'm not afraid; anyone can see that. I really don't want to come down.

The caretaker wrestles his way out a little farther and opens his arms wide. His solid torso bends slightly in the wind, his eyes are watering, the skin around the corners of his mouth is dry and cracked. I smell the cigarettes and beer. With his red nose, he looks like a clown. He stretches his pale hands out towards me, his breath suspended. Like a peacock's tail, his powerful arms describe a uniquely graceful welcoming gesture, tracing an arched bracket around his frozen face. I awake from my torpor, look at him gravely and suddenly recall his first name – and that Grandpa never once laughed at him. Taking a deep breath, I stretch out my skinny leg towards the caretaker.

On the day Mama lugs our heavy suitcase downstairs to the taxi in the courtyard, the children are sitting in the trees watching us. Olga isn't there. I try to catch hold of the handle on the side of the case, to give Mama a hand. Grandpa used to carry the case for her, now it's up to me. As we walk under the trees towards the car, Stas raises his hand in a farewell gesture.

'I'll be back when your hair's grown back!' I call out to him.

He spits out a cherry stone and laughs.

Translated from the German by Fiona Graham

Illustrations by Moni Port

A Trip to Town

Maria Parr

I'm going to tell you a story about a journey. Well, actually, I suppose it's more of a story about a non-journey, but that hardly matters, because it was Marie, my granny, who told it to me, and she was such a good storyteller.

Now that I think about it, it's a bit of a shame that you can't hear my granny tell you the story too. But you can try to pretend you're sitting on a kitchen chair and are about nine years old, can't you? Then you can imagine a granny sitting on the other side of the table.

My granny and I had almost the same name, Marie and Maria, and each of us was as much of a chatterbox as the other, even though neither of us experienced very much by way of excitement. I went to school and my granny stayed at home, but we still had so much to tell each other whenever we met that smoke would almost be coming out of our ears. So one day, at the kitchen table, my granny told me about a problem she'd once had when she went to school a long, long time ago.

Back then, my granny lived on a farm called Korshaug. It was so beautiful at that farm, because from there you could see all the way down the wide valley to the sea, where a boat could take you over to the town. But Granny had never been to town. Her family had neither the money nor the time to go there, unless there was some reason they absolutely, positively had to.

Granny was desperate for some reason they would absolutely, positively have to go, but it was no good. Her friends, on the other hand, all got to go into town, one by one. Even her best friend had been there.

'Oh,' I said, remembering how my own best friend had been all the way to India, while I had never even left Norway.

Of course, it was a bit strange that my granny hadn't been into town. It wasn't far. You could almost see the town from her house. But so many things were different back then. Nobody had cars, for example, and my granny and her brothers and sisters had to do a lot of work, so they couldn't just get up and head into town.

'Marie's strong,' the grown-ups said.

And she was. My granny had been as strong as a small bull, although I found that quite hard to believe, because the hands she used to serve me meatballs with gravy were not that strong. They were all skinny and wrinkly, like a couple of long Danish pastries with icing sugar on top. And the legs that stuck out below my granny's apron were so thin that sometimes I was scared they might snap right off. Granny was scared of the same thing, which is why she crossed the kitchen floor so slowly and carefully.

When I was there in the kitchen with her, I sometimes wondered whether Granny might have wanted to conjure back some of the strength she'd had as a child, especially when she needed to carry the heavy pot of boiled potatoes from the oven to the sink.

Whenever Granny did that, I always held my breath. I think you would've done the same. My mum thought that Granny should use a steamer, as it kept Granny's grown-up children awake at night worrying about all the boiling water she might drop. Granny would say 'mm-hmm' and nod, but as soon as Mum was out of sight, she'd fill the pot right up with water just like she'd always done. Meanwhile, I'd sit at the kitchen table, watching Granny frown with concentration as she dug her heels in, as if she were about to lift a horse. Then she'd lean her stomach against the worktop and swing the pot perilously through the air, before putting it down in the sink with a triumphant thud and slosh. The older Granny got, the louder the thud became, and I could just imagine how much she must have longed to be strong again.

But when she was young, it was the other way round. Back then, I think Granny often wished her strength would just make like a sock and get lost. After all, it's not much fun being strong if it means you've always got to do the heaviest work. Granny liked to bake, or to look after her younger siblings and help out in the house. But because she was strong, she was often sent off to the barn to shovel the muck and do other kinds of hard graft.

I wonder if it was when she was in the barn that Granny became so good at telling stories. She didn't like wearing those dirty clothes and those mucky boots, so she pretended she was in town shopping for some smart black shoes instead. While my strong little granny shovelled away, her imagination ran wild. The cows were posh ladies selling kringle pastries, coffee or shoes, and my granny raised her head, put on a posh voice and spoke to them.

'Good day, madam,' she said, shifting the muck like there was no tomorrow. 'I would like a pair of shiny black shoes, please.'

The cows had no idea what she was on about, as what did they know about town life anyway? But that didn't matter, because it was Granny who did all the lines.

As for her, she sure knew a few things about town life. In fact, it was quite extraordinary how much she knew. That best friend of hers was only too happy to tell people about it, especially if they asked the right questions. And Granny asked the right questions. She asked about the boat to town, about the shops and the people and their clothes, and her best friend told her everything. I can only imagine it would've been awful listening to it all, since my granny still hadn't been there herself, but she found it fascinating. The more she heard about town, the more it came alive in her mind. Eventually, Granny could picture every little bit of the town in her head.

Now you're probably thinking: 'Aren't you going to tell us about that journey that wasn't a journey?' You're probably thinking we're getting sidetracked, and you'd be quite right. But that's what it was like when Granny and I sat there talking in the kitchen. We'd go way off on a tangent, and then we'd come all the way back again. And that's what's just happened now too.

But you're right that we should get to the point. There's only one more important thing I should say, though, which is that of course my granny didn't go around telling everybody that she'd never been to town. She acted all nonchalant-like. After all, she knew that sooner or later there would be a reason she would absolutely, positively have to go there too. Besides, she'd decided to keep a low profile and talk about other things, because it was embarrassing not having been to town, as I think you'll understand. Probably the only person who knew was her best friend. You can trust best friends.

But then Granny got into a spot of bother at school. It was a perfectly ordinary day, and she was happy, because she liked being at school. There was no manure to shovel there, and no heavy work. Granny was especially fond of writing essays, and you can guess what the teacher gave them for homework that day: an essay to write. Granny sat up straight, and her eyes lit up with expectation as she looked towards the teacher's desk. What would they be asked to write about? The teacher peered over the top of his glasses. Granny held her breath.

'"A Trip to Town",' said the teacher. 'Your topic to write about is a trip to town.'

'Uh-oh,' I said.

'Mm-hmm,' said Granny, nodding.

What you've got to remember now is that school was important for Granny. She knew that she wasn't going to spend so many years at school, because that's what it was like in those days. Most people had to finish school after six or seven years and start working. Granny too. But that's another story. At that point she was still going to school, and she wanted to show everybody that not only was she strong, but that she had a good brain too.

But now she was in a sticky situation. Do you think Granny was going to go to the teacher and tell him she'd never been to town? Do you think she wanted all her classmates to find out that she'd never been there? No way. Not on your nelly. Nor was she going to go home and complain to her parents. Granny loved her parents, and she knew very well it wasn't their fault she'd never been to town. It was just the way things were.

So do you know what she did? She spent a long time pondering what to do, and when she'd finished all the other things she had to do at home that evening, she sat down and wrote at the top of the page, in nice, joined-up writing: 'A Trip to Town.'

If I'd been able to see my granny then, sitting over her jotter in the light of a paraffin lamp, I think she would've had almost exactly the same expression she had when she was about to lift up the pot of potatoes almost eighty years later.

She frowned in concentration, took a deep breath and got going.

And she started writing a story. Her pen screeched and scratched as she wrote all about the time she hadn't really gone to town to buy some shiny black shoes. So now everything my granny had longed for and dreamt of was coming in very handy. She wrote about this journey – a journey she'd never made – so vividly that you could smell the town. Everything her best friend had told her shone twice as brightly in my granny's mind, as she'd never been there herself.

'Well, how did it go?' I asked breathlessly.

My granny leant slightly forward over the kitchen table and looked at me triumphantly.

'I got ten out of ten,' she said, sticking her chin out just a little.

Then we laughed. Ten out of ten was the best mark you could get back in those days. Granny had concocted a story that knocked spots off all the rest.

Now you'll be thinking this was a story about almost nothing. And you'd be quite right. But this was the type of story Granny and I used to tell each other in the kitchen. We never experienced very much by way of excitement; neither she nor I did. I went to school and she stayed at home. And we never ran out of stories.

Translated from the Norwegian by Guy Puzey

Illustrations by Tony Ross

The Great Book Escape

Ævar Þór Benediktsson

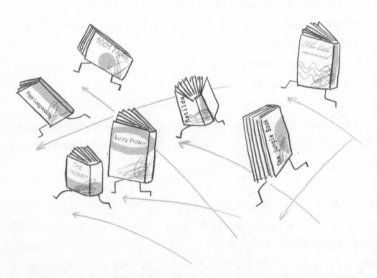

It was Monday at approximately 8:47 a.m. when Sigrun the librarian turned on the lights in the children's section only to discover that all of the bookshelves were completely empty.

The shelves startled Sigrun, because they'd had been tightly packed with children's books of all shapes and sizes only the day before, but now they looked like old friends who'd suddenly lost all of their teeth.

Sigrun's first reaction was to drop her Moomin mug. It was her favorite coffee cup, so letting it fall through the air was a very serious matter. The mug crashed when it hit the floor and broke into pieces, causing her coffee to splash all over the grey carpet and on her slippers.

Her next move was to open her mouth and close it again, four and a half times – as if she were a fish on dry land. The reasons behind this spasm were simple: Sigrun had too many questions circulating around her head at almost the exact same second, like an avalanche of thought. Here are a few of them:

Where are all the books?

Am I dreaming?

My coffee cup broke!

There's coffee on the floor!

Did I remember to turn off the stove?

(Observant readers will notice the last question doesn't really fit in with the rest, but we all know that it always comes up, no matter what we're doing.)

Instead of asking any of these questions aloud, however, Sigrun only let out a sound. It was a strange sound. A sound that she'd never made before in her entire life. It was a blend of sounds really, the type of gargle that little kids make when they're fussing, or the whine a car makes when refusing to start.

That might sound a little bizarre, but you have to understand that Sigrun the librarian loved children's books. She downright lived for them. She'd read all of the children's books in the collection more than once, every single one, and she couldn't imagine a world without them. If anybody had returned one of the children's books that they'd taken out and had accidently ripped a page, Sigrun would have blown up at them, and if anybody had damaged one of them in some way, Sigrun would have spent entire days meticulously repairing it.

Sigrun always arrived at the library before any of the other staff, and she always left last, only to rush home to sink into the children's books that she'd checked out herself that day. It didn't matter that she'd read them before – she could always lose herself in the story. She cried when she was supposed to cry, and burst into laughter at jokes that she'd heard countless times before. Sigrun the librarian wasn't really one to go out or try anything new (like, for example, putting pineapple on pizza or listening to music that had been composed in the last twenty-five years) and when she read something, she preferred to read something that she had read before and knew how it ended. That was safest.

Sigrun had definitely been at her shift last night. It was *her* who'd turned out the lights, which she now brought back to life. *She* was the last person in the area. And when *she* had clicked the lock, the section had still been full of children's books. She was certain of that!

But where are they, then?

Sigrun the librarian walked, shaking, through the barren stacks and stretched out her hand – as though she imagined that the empty shelves were merely a trick of the light and the books were, in reality, still there.

Nothing.

Then, suddenly, Sigrun the librarian heard a sound. It was a sound she had heard countless times before. A very distinctive sound that was impossible to imitate.

It was the sound of turning pages.

Sigrun the librarian looked around frantically. If there was a page turning somewhere in the library, that meant there had to be a book with pages to turn. Right? She scanned the shelves as quickly as she could – which was, as it turned out, very quick, because Sigrun was also a trained speed-reader.

Empty.

Finally, she looked down at the floor. And there it lay – a single sheet of paper crumpled under her right slipper. Sigrun had been so worked up about the empty bookshelves that she hadn't paid attention to anything else. She threw herself to the floor, grabbed on to the sheet of paper as if her life depended on it and lifted it to the light. Maybe the sheet concealed a top-secret secret message that could only be read by solving a sophisticated secret code, like in the Nancy Drew and Hardy Boys books. Maybe it was written in milk or invisible ink and you had to hold the sheet of paper up to a lamp or a candle to read what was on the page!

But that didn't turn out to be the case.

There were only a few words on the page, printed in a number of different fonts, like they'd been clipped out of any number of books and then glued to the page.

FIND us.
you KnoW where WE have BEen
YOU'll thank us LATER

Sigrun the librarian stared at the words. What in the world did it mean? She was completely baffled. Who was this 'us' that she should find? And where have 'they' been? She hardly knew anyone – certainly not enough people to constitute an 'us'. Her only friends were the children's books.

She got back up on her feet and slowly began to get her bearings. She peered at her Moomin mug, which still lay shattered on the floor, and shook her head.

'Best to sweep this up...' she muttered to herself. The cleaning supplies were in the little closet in the cellar under the stairs and she wanted to fetch them before anybody was there to see. Sigrun climbed down the stairs of the big library, puzzling over the riddle. Who had this note come from? Where had the books gone? Why should she thank them? Sigrun turned the doorknob of the storage closet under the stairs, pulled open the door and found herself facing a stack of books.

They were children's books! Children's books that Sigrun had read countless times before. Seven of them. There they were, neat and quiet, as if nothing could be more natural than seven of the most popular books of all time being stored in the closet under the old stairs.

'But...' Sigrun said to herself and felt a shudder of excitement run through her, 'of course you'd be here...' The books didn't answer – since they were just books. Anything else would have been absurd. All the same, Sigrun the librarian knew she was right. The hero of these books had grown up in a closet under the stairs. That's why they were here – because it couldn't have been otherwise. She was positive. That was what the note meant!

She grabbed up all seven Harry Potter books in her arms and stumbled with them up the stairs. The cleaning supplies could wait.

'Excellent,' said Sigrun the librarian to herself as she surveyed the next-to-empty-except-for-seven-books bookshelves in front of her. 'I know where you've been...' she said quietly and pursed her lips. Now she'd need to do her very best. Sigrun had read all of the children's books in the collection from cover to cover, and she felt certain that it was up to her to find them. She had found the note – that was her proof. She sighed deeply and took a gulp from a different Moomin mug (anyone who owns one Moomin mug owns at least three).

To tell the truth, she didn't like this at all. Because it was out of the ordinary it was also very disagreeable and beyond her comfort zone. But though it would surely be a bit of a nuisance to track down all the books that took place around the country, even that wasn't insurmountable. It was the books that took place out of the country that made her anxious. But what scared her most – still more than the idea of strange lands and uncertain endings – was what would happen if she were too late to find the books.

'Well and good,' she said again, even though nobody was really listening. 'You trusted in me. I won't let you down.' She gave a nod of her head in self-assurance and emptied her cup in one gulp. The knots in her stomach were little by little turning into butterflies.

* * *

Some of the books were no problem to find. All of the *Captain Underpants* books could be found, for example, in the nearest underwear department. In a desperate search for the fifth book in the series, Sigrun started to throw underpants to and fro, leaving a trail of undies in her wake. She didn't even try to explain what she was doing to the cashier, but instead strode away and pretended not to hear when he called after her.

It was a slightly bigger problem to find the books with more ambiguous titles, like *Demon Dentist* and *Awful Auntie*. Everyone knows there are too many demon dentists to count and even more awful aunties. Because of that, the search took longer than

Sigrun had anticipated. After an endless flurry of dentists offices and old folks' homes, Sigrun finally found the books (*Awful Auntie* had fallen behind the bed of an old woman who was particularly rude and the Demon Dentist turned out to be the old dentist that Sigrun had gone to when she was little – which she had, of course, expected from the beginning). She returned them to their proper place.

Sometimes Sigrun only found one book at a time. But in between her less successful ventures she often stumbled upon an entire pile. For example, all the young adult-novels (which were included in the kids' section) seemed to have no inclination to hide themselves, and so had gathered together at the nearest bus stop, where they just sort of hung around. Sigrun had to travel on all fifteen bus routes back and forth to rustle them back into the collection.

Time passed, and Sigrun's search continued. She had started to smile more than usual lately, and had more colour in her cheeks. This search game seemed to give her renewed purpose. She still had children's books on her mind, except this time she felt as if she was the one on *their* minds. Sometimes she merely strolled around and stumbled upon books (like, for example, when she found *Matilda* in the adult section of another library or when she went to a burial out in the countryside and saw a copy of *The Graveyard Book* next to a sinking headstone). But more often than not she needed to sit down and think. She needed to try to recall every single children's book she'd ever read in order to work out where each one might be… Sometimes that place was apparent – sometimes it was far from the case.

Each time she found a book, she carried it ceremoniously back to the children's section, carefully arranging it in alphabetical order. That was very important. It went slowly, but surely, and if someone who worked with her at the library asked what she was up to in the children's section, she said simply, *collection maintenance*. Because Sigrun was the most knowledgeable of anyone about that section, nobody dared to protest.

After she'd made three full circuits around the country and climbed one mountain (where the Norse sagas were waiting for her), she stopped finding any more books – no matter where she looked. That could mean only one thing: the time had come! She must travel to foreign lands.

Sigrun packed her passport in her suitcase and then gathered up clothes of all shapes and sizes and laid them in. She thought it was strange, and a little uncomfortable – but utterly thrilling.

Before she knew it, Sigrun was standing in the Klondike, with a copy of *Scrooge McDuck* in her hand. A few weeks later she stood beside a statue of the little mermaid in Copenhagen, where the adventures of Hans Christian Andersen were waiting for her. And she was just getting started. Sigrun thought to herself that the vast forest would be the perfect place to begin to look for fantasy novels and other similar stories, and it just so happened that she was exactly right. All of the Grimms' fairy tales, as if they'd just lain down for a rest, had settled themselves in the German tree branches and on the German riverbanks and were waiting with bated breath for her to come and find them.

The Adventures of Tintin were actually quite a bit of trouble, because they moved around so much. In one month, Sigrun the librarian was bundled up from head to toe in Tibet, and the next

thing she knew, she was suffocating from the humidity in South America. She had a nice stopover in the Norwegian forest, where Lilly the Lemming and Her Forest Friends were hiding away in a cute little bakery, and the week after that she found the adventures of Emil of Lönneberga in Katthult, hanging from a flagpole in Vimmerby, Sweden. Finding *1001 Nights* was easier said than done, because Sigrun started off by visiting the biggest city in Arabia, but ended up finding them buried in the sand right on the edge of a lush oasis. Days, weeks and months passed, but Sigrun never gave up! She knew exactly which books she still needed to find and she was going to find them all!

It took many years – but by the end of it, all of the stories were returned to the building. The final book that was missing, *The Hobbit*, Sigrun found waiting under her pillow when she returned from her world tour. The book, like Bilbo, clearly wanted to be home and not mixed up in any needless adventures.

* * *

Sigrun took a gulp of her coffee (from her third Moomin mug) and lifted it high into the air as if proposing a toast to the books. As if she were thanking them. She turned round to face a crowd of children who were waiting anxiously to come into the children's section. Finally, after all of these years, she was going to open it anew.

'Remember to be gentle with the books,' Sigrun said firmly. The children nodded. They were both excited and frightened of this heroic woman. They had heard all kinds of stories about her over the years. Some said that she had wrestled a crocodile to rescue a copy of *Peter Pan* from its jaws – others said that she had broken into a particularly fortress-like bank to get a hold of a very valuable edition of *Mary Poppins*.

'Remember that the best part of finishing a book is the knowledge that you can now read another,' she continued. The children nodded.

'And don't be surprised to find sand in the creases, or leaves, or even paragraphs bitten out of the books. They've been through a lot.' She smiled, but the children didn't dare do anything other than nod their heads.

'And now,' she continued, after a pause, gesturing towards the shelves, 'it's your turn. Time to go looking for some adventures of your own…'

Translated from the Icelandic by Meg Matich

Illustrations by Barbara Nascimbeni

Lady Night

Alaine Agirre

1 – The Three Sisters

There once was night, and there were also three sisters called Blanket, Coverlet and Quilt.

When the dark came, when the moon and her glow and everything woke, the sun, all shy, would hide until he found the courage to show himself again; that is to say until the following day. And like all children, when night arrived, Blanket, Coverlet and Quilt had to go to bed – do as their parents said. Be that as it may, the three sisters hated going to bed. One night when the moon's belly was full, Blanket was born; Coverlet

night when the stars played *twinkle-twinkle*, and
and off, and off and on; and finally, Quilt joined
ight sky was filled with clouds that looked like the
sea. Blanket enjoyed rubbing and caressing rough surfaces,
like the wooden table in the kitchen, strawberries, the cat's
tongue… Coverlet, on the other hand, liked drawing poetry on
the walls. And Quilt, finally, loved nothing more than to steal
the sounds of the neighbour's violin practice and compose
her own symphonies.

But there was one thing that all three, Blanket, Coverlet and
Quilt, had in common: they didn't like going to sleep at night.

2 – Hold Her Hand

'Blanket, hold Coverlet's hand,' Ama said every morning without
fail to the eldest sister, kissing her forehead. 'And you, Coverlet,
hold Quilt's,' she'd say then to the middle sister, kissing her cheek.

'And who will I hold on to?' Quilt would ask, preoccupied.

'You have the most important job of all, my love,' Ama answered
the little sister every morning without fail, kissing the dimple in
her chin: 'You must be careful and not get lost.'

And like this, holding each other by the hand, forming a step-
ladder of long manes of shiny hair, they would go to school.

3 – School

In school, they would learn one thing each day. In the early days,
at the beginning, when they were small, their heads were almost
empty and weighed nothing. But every day one thing would enter
their mouths, or their ears, or their nostrils – the way letters enter

postboxes, just like that. That's why bit by bit their heads were growing. And they learnt so, so, *so* much that...

'What if some day our heads explode?' Coverlet asked their teacher one morning.

'That won't happen,' the teacher replied, but seeing that Coverlet wasn't convinced they added: 'at least, not yet.'

'And what if all this learning obstructs our mouth-to-mind passageways?' Blanket asked after that.

'If that happens you'll have to take your learning through the nose,' answered the teacher after thinking for a while.

'And what if one day we come to class with a cold and our learning gets all mixed up with green snot?' asked Quilt nervously.

At times like this the teacher didn't know what to say and, fearing the onslaught of a crash of despair, would keep quiet and, shortly after, run away.

For these and a thousand other reasons, the teacher used to say the three sisters were very naughty. But come bedtime, that's when they would be really, really, *really* naughty.

4 – Bedtime

'Beeeeeedtime!' both parents shouted at once.

'It's late!' Aita said.

'You have to wake up early to go to school!' Ama chimed in.

But the sisters did everything they could to avoid going to bed: Blanket started running from one side of the room to the other; Coverlet did somersaults and vaults and twirls around the beds; and Quilt threw pillows hither and thither. And they carried on like this for a long time, making a din, causing chaos and commotion until their parents lost their minds.

'We don't want to go to bed!' yelled the three girls.

Huffing and puffing, with anger blowing out of their ears like smoke, the parents had to catch their daughters one by one to get them into their beds. But just as they got the first and second under the covers and reached for the third, the first one escaped her bed, and then so the did second one; this went on and on and on and on *and on*.

Until finally night arrived and, with her magic, filled the three sisters with sleepiness. Even if they'd wanted to keep their eyes open, they would close for a second – *wink* – and then open again – *wink* – but after that invariably they'd close again: like the stars, wink, wink. That is, in fact, why stars twinkle: they're winking.

And like this, their hard-fought battle lost, they'd fall asleep quite suddenly: one as she ran around, the other one while doing somersaults, vaults and twirls, and the third holding a pillow in her hands.

Ama and Aita, exhausted by now, would take Blanket, Coverlet and Quilt in their arms and put each into her bed.

5 – Fears

On that night, everything started just as it did every other night, with Aita reading them a fairy tale. It was *Sleeping Beauty* that night, a story about a princess who is put under a spell that keeps her asleep for ever. The three sisters, quite frightened, had a lot of questions for Aita:

'But *why* does the princess fall asleep?'

'But… but… why doesn't she wake up?'

'But… but… but… why doesn't someone save her?'

'It's OK, girls,' said Aita hoping to calm them down. 'The Sleeping Princess slept because a witch did some witchcraft on her, and she stayed asleep for a long time, because no one knew what to do. But then, one day, another princess came to the Kingdom, Princess Beauty, and gave her a kiss of love, and after that the Sleeping Princess woke up!'

But Aita's attempts at calming the girls backfired. Blanket, Coverlet and Quilt were more frightened than ever.

'And so if Princess Beauty hadn't come, then what... Sleeping Princess wouldn't wake up?'

'And... and... so if Princess Beauty had to fight a dragon before saving Sleeping Princess and lost the battle, then what: Sleeping Princess wouldn't wake up?'

'And... and... and so if Princess Beauty had arrived late, or hadn't arrived at all, then what: Sleeping Princess wouldn't wake up?'

The three girls were deep in the corridors of fear. As they took one step towards fear, and then another, and one more, they realized that fear got more frightening the farther they went.

Fear: of being imprisoned by the Night.

Fear: of being kidnapped by Sleep.

Fear: of never waking up again.

Fear, fear and fear.

And so that they wouldn't need Princess Beauty or anyone else to rescue them, so they wouldn't sink into perpetual sleep, so they wouldn't risk never waking up again, the three sisters decided to escape sleep for ever. But how?

6 – Sleep Avoidance

The three sisters unanimously decided to stop sleeping. Although they knew that every time Night came, Sleep would follow closely, and that it would be difficult to avoid them. This is why they devised the 'Sleep-Skipping Method'. The key to the method consisted in doing something special that would stop them from falling asleep.

'Tonight we'll dance through the night to avoid Sleep,' suggested Blanket.

And so they did. When their parents told them to go to bed, they obeyed and diligently slipped into their beds and pretended to be falling asleep.

'Sleep well, princesses,' whispered their parents into their ears, and they gave each girl a kiss.

But, as soon as Aita and Ama were out of the room and the door was closed, the girls leapt out of their beds and started dancing. Waving their arms, shaking their hips, twisting their waists and moving their heads right and left, they danced and danced. The clock's hands moved forward and got tired and bored of the sisters dancing for so long, and started moving forward and backward and left and diagonally. But suddenly the Sun got lost in the darkness of the Night, and then the Moon, so elegant and so grand, so fine and so exquisite, brought Sleep along.

'Careful, girls!' shouted one sister.

'It's coming! Sleep is coming!' screamed another.

'Stay alert!' warned the third.

And they continued to dance with even greater determination, waving their arms, shaking their hips, twisting their waists and moving their heads right and left; drops of sweat dripped down their cheeks, tickling their faces.

But it was all for nothing.

Sleep came and caught them.

Early in the morning, they were very relieved to see that they'd been able to wake up.

'But it can't happen again,' said the eldest sister.

'We have to skip sleep,' added the middle one.

'Otherwise, one day we might not wake up,' said the youngest, 'and on that night…'

'Tonight, to escape Sleep, we'll pretend to be monkeys all night long,' suggested Coverlet.

As soon as their parents had kissed their cheeks and closed the door behind them, they jumped out of their beds and started acting like monkeys. They jumped between the beds and, like monkeys, dragged their arms and thumped their chests shrieking, as if they were in the jungle. And they spent such a long time doing this, even the clock's hands got tired and bored of moving forward. And when they started moving backward and forward and left and diagonally, Night came.

'Caaaaaareful!' – shouted the three sisters at once.

And they played monkeys even more enthusiastically than before, trying to escape Sleep. But it was all for nothing.

Sleep came and captured them.

'Tonight, to avoid Sleep, we'll play at being Native Americans all night,' Quilt proposed.

And that's what they did when their parents went to bed. They formed a circle and, turning this way and that, they skipped and danced like Native Americans, and war-whooped with their hands in front of their mouths. They did this for a long time; so long that the clock's hands, tired and bored and angry with the three sisters, decided to stop. At that moment, Night came through the window, dressed in darkness and the twinkle of stars. And with her came Sleep.

'Oh, nooooooo!' shouted the three sisters at once.

They started to play at being Native Americans even more energetically than before. But it was all for nothing. Sleep came and entrapped them for ever.

7 – The Shadow

They'd never seen it before that very moment. Sleep looked like a shadow: a child's shadow, to be precise. It moved quickly, with little quivers, rays of life, flying here and there, as if aiming to wipe away the dust of reality. And everywhere it went, it left a glittery trail that made everyone want to follow.

Quilt did just that. Enchanted by the sparkle, mouth agape, she followed Shadow. As she walked, she tripped on a pillow and fell on the floor. Before Blanket and Coverlet could do anything (they were also enchanted, as if under a spell), Shadow approached the youngest sister and offered her a hand. The sparkle that came off Shadow was so, so beautiful that Quilt offered her hand too. Shadow pulled at it ever so softly and, in a second, the child's feet floated a few centimetres over the ground. Shadow kept floating up, slowly, till they were so high that Quilt could touch the ceiling with her free hand.

'Look, sisters, I'm flying!' shrieked Quilt, delighted.

Blanket and Coverlet were looking at her with her mouths open, flabbergasted. A mixed feeling of fear and dazzlement kept them firmly locked in their places. They didn't know what to do:

should they hold Quilt by the ankles to help her come down, or should they also…

'Give me your hand, Coverlet!' said Quilt to her sister.

Wavering, in doubt, unsure what to do, Coverlet stopped thinking and raised a hand. Quilt took it and she started to float too, joining her little sister and Shadow. They started circling from one end of the room to the other, rolling around, leaping, somersaulting, pirouetting… They went on like this, twirling around in a mad whirlwind until they were dizzy, while Blanket stared at them from the ground.

'Blanket!'

'Come join us!'

Shocked, shell-shocked, in shock, Blanket raised her hand and held Coverlet's tightly. In that instant, a gust of air opened the windows, and Night's dew drenched the entire room. Dewdrops caressed their skin; but, despite this, Quilt, Coverlet and, finally, Blanket, followed Shadow and flew out of the window and into the Night.

Up and up they went, towards the stars, leaving the song of the street crickets behind. Quilt thought that under the clouds darkness would be absolute were it not for the streetlights and the house lights below. Blanket thought that those little lights looked like tiny embers, like ants in a deep sleep. Coverlet grabbed a baby star with her free hand, stealing it from the night sky, and put it in her pyjama pocket without saying anything.

'We're flying!'

'To the sky!'

'Here we go!'

Following Shadow, holding tight on to each other's hands, they travelled on, until they reached the shelter of the sky. Every now and then they went through misty clouds and, on those occasions, the three sisters would close their eyes and mouths and stop breathing for a few seconds, fearful of swallowing a bit of cloud. But as they went up and the clouds increased, they realized the air smelt more and more like sweets. And, suddenly, just like that, Quilt opened her mouth and gulped a chunk of cloud.

'Coverlet, Blanket – taste the clouds!'

Her two sisters followed her advice and immediately started shouting with joy.

'They're candyfloss!'

The three sisters and Shadow went up, and up, and uuuuuuup… It felt like they were swimming, they moved their legs like frogs, *open-close*, *close-open*. The air hugged their skin, made their hair float as if it were underwater. Even though the atmosphere was cold, it felt warm to them.

And they went on like this, until they landed on the surface of a very dense and chubby cloud.

8 – On the Cloud

As they paused on top of the cloud, they let go of each other's hands. And then, after a curtsy, Shadow left them. Blanket, Coverlet and Quilt were on their own, like Night in her dress of darkness and stars.

They ate chunks of sweet cloud until their bellies were full, their mouths and hands were a mess and their fingers stuck together.

'So yummy! And I can eat as much as I like: it doesn't make my belly ache,' said Quilt.

'I'm full,' said Coverlet, brushing away bits of cloud still stuck to her pyjamas.

'And now what?' asked Blanket.

Although they didn't know what would happen next, they weren't worried or afraid. They knew that nothing bad could ever happen in the dream they were in, that they were safe.

'Watch out!' shouted Blanket, throwing a cloudball at their sisters. It shattered into a thousand pieces and fell on them like snow. They raised their hands and arms, opened their mouths and, looking up, started to turn and turn under a mist of soft cloud flakes. After a cloudball fight, they started walking like astronauts, in giant leaps that took them from one end of the cloud to another, bobbing in the air. Truth is, the laws of gravity and reality were suspended in that world.

'Girls!' shouted Coverlet to her sisters. 'Did you hear that?'

All three sisters paid close attention then, placing their hands behind their ears, waiting to hear something. And, all of a sudden, they started to hear an echo that came from far away. Little by little it grew, in a crescendo: at first it was an orchestra of string instruments, then the flutes and clarinets came in and, finally, they heard trumpets and trombones. As the music in the air grew, Blanket and Coverlet, holding each other, began to dance. Quilt started to conduct the invisible orchestra, waving her arms in the air. Who knows how much time they spent like that, dancing, twirling, waving their arms, moving their legs, bouncing in the air and being one with the music. Until that magical music grew dimmer and dimmer. Until they heard the voice.

9 – Lady Night

'Good night,' said the voice.

'Who are you?' asked the eldest sister, very curious.

They couldn't see anyone around because it was so, so dark.

'I can't see anything!' said the youngest, looking right and left. It was so, so dark.

'I've got an idea!' replied the middle sister: 'Let's switch on the Moon to see what's around us.'

And, as soon as she said that, the Moon came alive and switched itself on: it radiated this blinding white light. Though it hurt their eyes to begin with, they were now able to see their surroundings.

But there was no one there after all.

'Good evening,' spoke a deep voice that came from far away but was perfectly loud and clear.

'Who are you?' asked the three sisters at once.

'You know who I am,' replied the voice. 'I'm Lady Night.'

Blanket, Coverlet and Quilt were dumbstruck.

10 – The World of Dreams

'Where are you?'

'We can't see you!'

'I am here and there, there and here,' answered Lady Night. 'Since I am Night, I inhabit many places: Darkness, the Moon, the Stars, the Shadows…'

'And what do you want?'

'I'd like to know why you're running away from my friend Sleep,' answered the voice.

'We're afraid of you and your friend Sleep,' Coverlet confessed.

'Why are you scared of us?'

'Because you're dark,' said Quilt in a whisper.

'That's what the Moon and Stars are for; so you don't get lost, not even in the darkest moments,' said Lady Night calmly, peacefully.

'But you're very quiet too…' said Blanket accusingly.

'That's what Crickets are for; so you know where you are, even in the quietest moments.'

'The truth is we're afraid of falling asleep for ever, like the Sleeping Princess…' admitted Coverlet.

'You can relax: Sleep won't hold you hostage – at least, not for ever,' explained Lady Night. 'As long as you continue to dream that you're awake, you'll wake from your deep sleep every morning.'

'But we don't want to go home!'

'We want to stay here!'

'For ever!'

'You can't stay in the World of Dreams for ever – at least, not for now. But you can come every night, together with Sleep.'

'Who *is* Sleep?' asked Coverlet, very curious.

'The Shadow who brought you all the way here is Sleep. It joins me at the end of the day, and brings all the children of the world to the World of Dreams.'

'So, if we go to bed every night without fail, we'll be able to come back here?'

'Of course. And now I must leave: a new day is about to be born.'

The three sisters looked far ahead, and over there, in the distance, in the sky's farthest corner, they could see the first rays of the Sun. The Stars were getting shy, and the Moon, very sleepy, was beginning to switch off.

'And remember, don't be afraid of Night, or Sleep.' And with those words, Lady Night disappeared.

11 – With the Rays of the Sun

The window was open, and the light of the Sun filled the whole room with warmth.

'Good morning, girls!' said Ama, pulling back the girls' covers to help them wake up.

But the three sisters were still half-asleep. They didn't want to escape the World of Dreams; they wanted to stay there for a little bit longer…

'Ama…'

'Five more minutes…'

'Please…'

They couldn't forget how Sleep had flown them to the World of Dreams; how delicious the clouds had been; how it had felt up there in the sky, on top of a cloud, dancing to music that came from nowhere; how the Moon had switched on and then off; how they'd talked with Lady Night…

But, how had they returned home?

'Did you sleep well?' asked Aita.

And then they understood.

'We fell asleep,' said Blanket, very sad. 'It was all a dream.'

'So it's not true that we flew all the way to that cloud,' added Coverlet with a frown.

'And Lady Night and Sleep are not real…' finished Quilt, sounding sad.

As they were putting on their dressing gowns and slippers, Blanket felt something strange in her pyjama pocket. She put her hand in it, and when she pulled out what was inside, she was almost blinded. Because what she was holding was the little star she had robbed from the night sky as they flew up and up towards the cloud.

12 – Don't Be Afraid

Ever since that day, every evening at dusk, as soon as Night arrived, Blanket, Coverlet and Quilt ran to bed even before their parents asked them to. They placed the star they had robbed from the night sky on the bedside table so as not to get lost in the darkness, and left the window open so they could hear the crickets' song.

And like this, every night without fail, they waited to be carried to the World of Dreams. As soon as they dived into the sweetness of Sleep they flew all the way to meet Lady Night, and switch on the Moon, and steal some Stars, and eat some tasty clouds and dance to the music that came from nowhere and everywhere.

They never again feared they might fall asleep for ever; in fact, as they had been told by Lady Night – in other words, by me myself – so long as they continued to dream they were awake, there was no need to worry about any of that.

And you too, little child, don't be afraid of going to sleep. Come to me. Let Sleep bring you to the World of Dreams, because, you know, the dreams that don't come true while you're awake live here for ever.

Translated from the Basque by Amaia Gabantxo

Illustrated by Cato Thau-Jensen

Journey to the Centre of the Dark

David Machado

I was sleeping and I woke up when I heard my sister whispering to me. She's only five and I'm seven, so my main mission is to help her and teach her and protect her, and I go whenever she needs me. I opened my eyes but couldn't see anything. It was still night-time, and the room was really dark. I felt her hand on my arm and I asked:

'What happened?'

'A bad dream,' my sister replied.

I remembered all the bad dreams I'd ever had, and a shiver ran down my spine.

'It's gone now,' I explained.

'There were strange noises and shadows,' my sister said.

'I know. But it's gone now,' I said again.

'And monsters. Lots of monsters. Big ones and small ones and ones with claws and dirty teeth. They were ugly and horrible.'

All of a sudden I didn't want to be there, talking to my sister with the light off. And I know I'm seven already, but even so, sometimes I still get scared. Especially of monsters. Of course, I didn't tell my sister that. I wanted her to believe I was brave and that she could count on me for anything.

'Wait,' I said, 'I'm going to turn the light on.'

'You can't do that,' my sister said, frightened.

'Why not?'

'Because of the monster.'

'What monster?'

'The monster that's here next to me.'

When she said that I was so scared my tummy hurt.

'There's no monster,' I told her.

But, to tell the truth, I wasn't entirely sure. The darkness in the room was so black that, if there really was a monster next to my sister, there was no way I'd be able to see it.

'It's one of the monsters from my dream,' she said. 'It followed me and now it doesn't know how to get back to the other monsters.'

I stayed still and quiet for a little while, trying to listen for the monster's breathing in the middle of the silence. I couldn't hear anything. So I asked:

'And why can't I turn the light on?'

'He wouldn't like it,' my sister replied. 'You know what monsters are like. He might even eat us.'

I looked into the dark: the biggest monster in the world could be in there and I wouldn't be able to see it! All the same, I was sure what she was saying was impossible. So I said:

'Monsters don't come out of dreams.'

'Right,' said my sister. 'But the dream hasn't finished yet.'

I laughed and said:

'But if you're here talking to me, how can the dream not have finished?'

'This is part of the dream, silly! You're *in* my dream.'

Maybe she was teasing me. And I always know when she's teasing me because she opens her eyes really wide and the corner of her mouth wobbles a little bit. But I couldn't see her face so I wasn't sure. Could you really get inside someone else's dream?

'I know I'm awake,' I said.

'No,' she said, 'you just *think* you're awake. That's just what happens in dreams. You think you're awake but you're not.'

She was right: that's what happens in dreams. But I didn't want to believe her.

'This isn't a dream,' I said loudly and confidently.

I felt my sister's hand covering my mouth.

'Don't talk so loud,' she said. 'You'll scare the monster and then he'll eat us.'

'There's no monster here,' I whispered. 'You're not dreaming.'

She didn't say anything for a few seconds, and then, as if she'd discovered the biggest secret in the Universe, she said:

'Maybe you're the one who's dreaming.'

'No one's dreaming.'

'What about the monster?'

'What's the monster got to do with it?'

'I have to help him get back to the other monsters.'

'Really?'

'Yes. You don't want him to stay here in our room for ever, do you?'

'No, I don't.'

'So you have to come with me.'

'Me? Why?'

'Because I'm only five and I'm scared of taking the monster back on my own. But you're seven and you're not scared of anything.'

It wasn't true: I was so scared I could hardly breathe. And I didn't want to go and take the monster back to the other monsters.

But I couldn't tell her that. She needed me to be strong and brave. So I asked:

'Where are the other monsters?'

'In the centre of the dark,' said my sister.

'What's the centre of the dark?'

'The centre of the dark is where the dark is so dark that even your thoughts disappear and the only thing left is being scared.'

I didn't want to go to the centre of the dark. However, if my sister was sure and there really was a monster in our room, that was what we had to do.

'Why can't the monster go on his own?' I asked.

'You know what monsters are like,' my sister said. 'They like company.'

'I've never heard anyone say that about monsters.'

'But it's true. At least, that's what the monsters *I* know are like.'

I tried to think of other solutions, something I could say so we didn't have to take the monster to the centre of the dark. The only thing I could think of was that I didn't know the way to the centre of the dark. I told my sister that, and she replied:

'No problem, I know the way. It's over there.'

'Where?'

'Where I'm pointing.'

I couldn't see her finger, of course. So she grabbed my hand and said:

'Come on!' And then, straight away, she added, 'But don't let go of my hand.'

I carefully got out of bed. The darkness was so thick that for a moment I imagined the floor wasn't there. Then my feet touched the wood and I stood still until I felt my sister tugging my hand. That was how our journey into the centre of the dark began.

For the first few minutes, we walked in silence. I was so scared that I didn't want to hear the sound of my own voice. We turned left and then right and then left again and we didn't hit the bedroom wall, or bump into any furniture, and I thought that maybe we weren't in the room any more. Maybe we weren't even in our house. Suddenly, I remembered the monster. My sister said she was holding the monster's hand too, and he was walking beside her.

We carried on like that, the three of us, until my sister shouted:

'Watch out!'

'What happened?' I asked, frightened.

'You were about to fall off the cliff.'

'What cliff?'

'This cliff, the one in front of us. And you know what: there's fire down there.'

I felt dizzy and held tight to my sister's hand so I wouldn't lose my balance.

'I can't see anything,' I said.

'Of course you can't,' she said, laughing quietly. 'It's all dark.'

We carried on. After some time, she leant in close to my ear and whispered:

'Did you hear that?'

'What?'

'It sounded like someone howling.'

I stayed still, listening.

'I can't hear anything,' I said.

'It must be the wolves,' my sister explained.

'Which wolves?'

'The wolves that eat frogs and live in the woods.'

'Which woods?'

'The woods behind the wizard's house.'

'Which wizard?'

'The wizard who likes turning people into frogs.'

As she was telling me this, I was so scared that for a moment my heart stopped beating.

'How do you know all that?'

'I already told you, silly. This is my bad dream, and I know what happens in my bad dreams.'

'And you're not scared?'

'No, because you're here with me.'

My sister needed me there, but I didn't know if I could go on.

'Is it far?' I asked.

'No. We'll be there in about three days.'

'THREE DAYS?!'

'Don't shout,' whispered my sister, annoyed. 'If the ghosts hear us, they'll come after us to take us down underneath the dark.'

'What is there underneath the dark?'

'The same as here. But all upside down.'

I thought this was the scariest bad dream I'd ever been in. And then I had an idea.

'If this is a dream,' I said, 'why don't you try to wake up?'

'Because that's one of the problems with bad dreams: it's *really* hard to get out of them.'

Once again, she was right. And I didn't want to stay there another three days. But I also couldn't go back and leave my five-year-old sister behind. So we carried on.

111

We walked for a long time. My sister led the way and sometimes warned me not to tread on the snakes or step in the dirty puddles filled with piranhas. At a certain point, she smelt a disgusting smell and said we had to hide quickly because some ogres were coming. We huddled behind some rocks until they'd gone past and there was nothing left but the awful smell wafting on the breeze. Later on we crossed a desert where – my sister explained – many centuries ago, a witch had cast a sadness spell. My sister started crying.

'What's the matter?' I asked.

'I'm really sad. This spell is making me really sad. And the monster too. He's crying – look.'

I couldn't see the monster crying in all that darkness. But the truth is I was starting to feel sad and like I wanted to cry too. We ran to get out of there quickly and escape the spell. We ran until my sister said:

'I don't feel sad any more. We can stop.'

'Do you think it's been three days yet?' I asked, struggling to catch my breath.

'It's been twenty-two.'

'Really?'

'Yes. That's the other problem with bad dreams: you never really know how long a day lasts.'

'Is it still far to go?'

'No,' she said, 'we're here. The centre of the dark is right there.'

But, just as she said that, I felt her hand letting go of mine.

'What are you doing?'

'It's not me,' she shouted in the dark. 'It's the monster. He's pulling me into the centre of the dark.'

I waved my arms in front of me trying to find my sister's hand.

'Where are you?'

'Here.'

'I can't see you.'

'I'm here. But the monster is pulling me really hard. Help me…'

And then, all of a sudden, her voice disappeared. I called her name. My throat was so full of fear, though, that my voice came out too weak to cross the dark. I walked back and forth with my arms out, hoping to find her, but all I found was darkness. I was so scared that all my thoughts disappeared and the only thing left was fear. And then I knew I was in the centre of the dark.

I stayed still and quiet, not knowing what to do, as if the fear was holding me prisoner. The darkness was enormous. Inside it there was space for all the bad dreams in the world. Somewhere in that black place, lost and afraid, was my sister. But I had to find her, because she was my sister and she was only five, and because my mission is always to go when she needs me.

I called her again. Once. Twice. Three times. Little by little, my voice pushed the fear away, it came out of my mouth and echoed in the darkness around me. And, suddenly, I felt my sister's hand grabbing mine again and I heard her saying quietly:

'Don't shout. You'll wake the monsters up.'

I felt so relieved that, for a moment, the darkness seemed less dark.

'Sorry,' I said. 'But I couldn't find you and I was scared. Weren't you scared?'

'Of course not. I knew you were going to find me.'

'Where's the monster?'

'He lay down to sleep with the other monsters.'

'So can we go back to our room now?'

'Yes,' my sister said, yawning sleepily.

'You can't go to sleep yet,' I said. 'We've still got a twenty-two-day journey ahead of us.'

'No. The journey from the centre of the dark back to our room is always much quicker. Come on.'

She tugged my hand. Then we took two steps and she said:

'We're here.'

'Really?'

'Yes. You can turn the light on now.'

I turned the light on. The room appeared around us. My sister got into her bed. I got into mine. Just in case, I left the light on. I waited until my sister went to sleep, and then I went to sleep too.

Translated from the Portuguese by Lucy Greaves

Illustrations by Benji Davies

Dagesh and Mappiq
Are Friends

Jana Šrámková

Meet Dagesh. Dagesh sits on the ground, poking a stick in a molehill.

Dagesh is a naughty boy. Who is he naughty to? Almost everyone. He makes mischief and gobbles up whatever he can find. Dagesh is a field mouse.

During the day, he has all kinds of fun. There's always someone to laugh at, someone with supplies to eat, and someone to bite on the thumb. During the day, he can act up all he likes. But at night-time Dagesh battles with boredom.

What now? Everyone else is tucked away at home, humming and playing cards. Sometimes they laugh and other times they read exciting stories. The sweet aroma of pumpkin soup wafts up from the dens in the hillside.

Only Dagesh is all alone. He stares up at the round moon, tugging on his whiskers.

That's what you get! the crow caws, circling over the hushed field like a night watchman. *If you weren't such a pain in the neck, you might have friends!*

What does Dagesh say to that? He thumbs his nose at the crow. And then? He goes on staring at the moon, tugging on his whiskers.

Fine then, Dagesh decides after the crow has gone. He can't stand the silence. Starting tomorrow, he will turn over a new leaf. Instead of making fun of the other animals, he'll make friends with them.

But with whom? Everyone's already taken. And besides, as soon as they see Dagesh the field mouse, they zip inside their burrows. They all know what he's like.

It's night-time and Dagesh is all alone again. Even the moon is slipping away. What a pain in the neck.

And meet Mappiq. Mappiq doesn't know Dagesh, so he doesn't run away. He just moved here from the hill next door and is still learning his way around. Mappiq is a ground squirrel.

Well, aren't you a funny-looking mouse? Dagesh says, making a face. He looks the newcomer up and down. *Your cheeks are fat as a rat's, heh heh*. Then he remembers his decision. *But never mind. You want to come and play?*

117

What's the game? Mappiq asks warily.

It's called playing at being friends, Dagesh says.

And so they play.

That night, Dagesh is so tired out from playing, he doesn't even notice how much the moon has shrunk.

See you on the pirate ship tomorrow, he tells Mappiq. *And don't be late. We sail with the cock's crow!*

What if there isn't a favourable wind? Mappiq asks.

Then you'll just have to row, Dagesh says, rubbing his little paws.

Oh, right, says Mappiq.

They wave goodbye to each other and go to sleep.

The next day there is no wind, so they make a knight's suit of armour out of blades of straw. Plus swords and shields and lances. Then they launch into battle.

Charge! they cry, armour agleam, raising their swords in the evening sun as they dash headlong through the field at each other. They lower their visors and narrow their eyes.

Pow! Pow! Mappiq suddenly cries. Dagesh topples to the ground, dead, but then shouts:

What do you think you're doing, Mappiq? We're knights!

Not any more, says Mappiq, shaking his head. *Now we're playing cowboys instead.*

They play again the next day, and the day after that, and again and again, day after day. It is all they know how to do.

You know, I don't think we're even just playing any more, Dagesh suddenly realizes one day. *I think we're really friends.*

118

Stop thinking and drive! Mappiq shouts.

They are heading into a sharp turn in a Formula 1 race. Apparently Monte Carlo.

Look, Mappiq. A full moon. Let's go dance in the glade!

All right! Mappiq cries joyfully. Then suddenly he gets worried: *What if that's just for girls, though?*

Their mood plummets.

The moon is pale, the grass in the glade smooth as silk, and the trees murmur an evening song.

So what? Who cares, anyway? Dagesh suddenly bellows.

His words carry through the night, tree to tree, and he is absolutely right.

So Dagesh and Mappiq jump for joy and dance to the full moon until morning.

Then, one day, a storm cloud floats across the sky.

Go away, storm! Dagesh shouts at it. *Today we're going to cross the Sahara!*

Get lost! Mappiq threatens the storm. *The camels are saddled and ready to go!*

But the storm won't listen. It just keeps on getting darker and darker, ruffling the sky over the field.

Listen, Mappiq, Dagesh whispers. *I've got a better plan. Let's play command the wind and the rain.*

They clear their throats importantly.

Go ahead and rain already, Dagesh says, shaking his fist at the storm cloud.

Please, Mr Storm, would you be so kind as to give us some rain? Mappiq requests politely.

119

Thunder! they urge it. *Lightning!*

And the storm obeys their every word. They play cards as they take their afternoon tea and watch from their warm shelter, rejoicing at what a good job they have done.

Hey, Dagesh, would you go on a really long trip with me?

Summer is coming to an end. The wind smells of adventure, ruffling their fur. Dagesh and Mappiq stand amid the stubble field, staring into each other's eyes. Finally Dagesh nods yes.

I knew it, Mappiq says excitedly. *Come on, let's fly into space!*

So off they fly. First up, then down. They take a right-hand turn at Jupiter and circle twice around the Milky Way. They finally come to a landing just in time for dinner.

So what are we going to do today?

Today we're going to conquer Troy, Mappiq beams. *You will be the mighty Hector and I will be Achilles.*

But I don't know that story, Dagesh says, squirming with embarrassment.

I can tell it to you if you want, says Mappiq. *Better sit down. This will take a while.*

Three beautiful goddesses had an argument over an apple, Mappiq begins. He tells Dagesh all about Paris and the beautiful Helen of Troy, and how twelve hundred ships sailed forth to make war on them. It was such a long war that the sun travelled all the way across the sky over their heads, and still the ancient city of Troy withstood the enemy's attacks. Dagesh listens breathlessly to the tale of the Trojan horse. By the time proud Troy has fallen and the last heroes have returned safely home, Mappiq has a sore throat.

All because of an apple? Dagesh whispers in amazement.

And all of a sudden they both get a terrible craving for one, so they roll a nice juicy apple out of the ground squirrel's burrow and chop it in half with the sharp sickle of the moon, delighted that there isn't any goddess around they have to share it with.

The next thing they know, the weather is turning cold, the wind is whistling through the field, and Mappiq's no fun any more.

Hey, Mappiq, are you sure you're not overeating? says the field mouse, bouncing around the ground squirrel. *Hey, Mappiq, why don't you come and play? We can be castaways. Look, a boat on the horizon!*

But Mappiq won't listen. He just runs back and forth, stuffing himself silly.

Hey, Mappiq, stop eating – you're getting fat! You won't fit in the racing car!

Stay out of my way, Mappiq squeals, biting into another ear of corn. *If I don't eat enough, come spring it'll be the end of me. Don't you get it?*

But Dagesh doesn't get it.

Goodnight! Mappiq cries at noon one day, trundling off to his hole.

What are you talking about? says Dagesh. *It's still morning!*

Winter hibernation, buddy. Come on, it's high time!

Dagesh just stares in bewilderment. *Do ground squirrels sleep all winter long?*

Of course! Don't field mice?

121

Don't go, pleads Dagesh.

I have to, yawns Mappiq.

You'll be hungry!

No, I won't. That's why I ate so much.

But… what if I miss you?

Mappiq has no answer for that. He just shrugs sadly.

The time has come to say farewell:

Bye, then.

Goodbye.

Dagesh helps seal up the ground squirrel's burrow with dry grass.

Can I at least come and wake you every once in a while? he asks Mappiq once there is no longer anything left between them but a little crack.

If you do, it'll be the end of me, Mappiq says, shaking his head. *You can manage till the spring, can't you, buddy?*

Dagesh nods. What choice does he have?

Goodnight, Mappiq.

Dagesh sits on the ground, poking a stick in a molehill.

Dagesh the field mouse is all alone. Just like at the start of the summer.

But it isn't the same.

Deep underground, Mappiq's heart is beating for Dagesh. It's just a tiny little squirrel heart, but to Dagesh it feels like the whole hill is thumping.

Dagesh is all alone, but he isn't making mischief now. Where would he find the time? He's got a job to do.

He takes out the old knight's armour, patching it up and polishing it. He's going to stand guard over Mappiq's burrow.

Fifty paces there, about-face, fifty paces back. Atten-shun!

At ease.

Snow is one thing Dagesh has never liked much. It's hard work searching for food beneath the snow. And cold on the paws!

But this year Dagesh is glad for the snow. He welcomes the first flakes with a wild jungle dance, stomping around in the powder until the snow starts to pour down from the sky.

The snow covers the frozen soil like a down quilt. Now it will be nice and warm underground. Dagesh pushes a whole mound of snow over to Mappiq's burrow, piling it up till it looks like an igloo.

Such a sunny winter's day! But where has Dagesh got to? He's sitting on the hillside, tugging on his whiskers.

I never realized being a friend was such hard work.

If only I weren't so all alone.

Dagesh misses his friend. The exploratory outings. The expeditions, the flights, the cruises. But he can't travel now, that's for sure. He's needed here.

He pulls his cap down over his ears and does a few squats to warm himself up. With a leap in between. But what then?

I can't believe I didn't think of it before, Dagesh says to himself, rolling the snow into a big lump. *I'll build a snowman! Then he can stand guard when I go to sleep.*

It was cold going and it's taken him almost a week, but now a statue of a field mouse, made of snow and larger than life, stands in front of Mappiq's igloo. And next to it a ground squirrel, just as it should be.

A true work of art! But what good was such a beautiful thing when Mappiq wasn't there to see it? Couldn't he come out, at least once, for a little while… Maybe just knock on the door and see if he pokes his head out? Hesitantly, Dagesh begins burrowing into the snow.

Shame on you, field mouse! a crow caws at him from overhead.

Dagesh quickly smooths the snow back over again. Now he will be ashamed the whole time until Christmas.

It's time! Christmas is here! Dagesh pulls a fir seedling over to the igloo and decorates it with sweets. When night falls, he lies beneath the stars, looking for the route that he and Mappiq followed when they flew around the Milky Way.

Look, Dagesh, a falling star! Make a wish!

Dagesh wishes that winter wouldn't drag on so long.

Stop stomping around like that, you clumsy oaf! You'll wake him up! Dagesh goes chasing after a deer who has come out of the woods to savour what's left of the candied walnuts decorating the tree.

Dagesh pulls his pistols from their holsters and fires into the air. The roebuck eyes him watchfully, noticing the shiny sheriff's star pinned to his chest. Then turns around and runs off into the woods.

Finally, Dagesh exhales. He places his ear to the igloo, worried that he might have woken his friend. The snow is covered with deer's hoofprints. What a relief! He can't hear a thing.

He never would have guessed before that silence could make him so happy.

The moon waxes, wanes and waxes, and still Dagesh stands guard. Ever on the alert, walking, running, on his belly, his back, his side, asleep... Huh?

What happened? Who did that? I barely drift off and somebody comes along and ruins my sculpture! The field-mouse snowman has crumbled against the ground-squirrel snowman's back.

Then suddenly it dawns on him: *Hurray! It's melting!*

Dagesh hurls his hat into the clouds for joy. He won't be needing that any more.

Then a week later, he takes off his scarf. The first leaves sprout from the earth.

It's spring, Mappiq, whoopee! Dagesh shouts himself hoarse, jumping and stomping around the burrow.

But still no sound from the hole in the ground.

Where are you, buddy? Are you all right?

Dagesh is tired out from the winter. He's fallen asleep on patrol out of sheer worry and exhaustion.

Look at the knight in his threadbare armour, snoring away beside the burrow, curled up in a ball.

Get up, Dagesh! he suddenly hears a voice beside him. *Do you never do anything but sleep?*

The two friends jump for joy, hugging, shouting and rolling around on the ground. They do handstands and somersaults, running and falling, laughing and shrieking, poking each other and wrestling and boxing, falling down flat on their backs and kicking their feet till they run out of breath.

They can't care less what the deer thinks, as she comes out of the woods to graze, because this is a glorious day, the two of them are together again, and awake, and *hip hip hooray!*

Come on, Mappiq. I made you breakfast, Dagesh says once he finally comes to his senses again.

Mappiq is happy to eat. After his winter hibernation he's practically nothing but skin and bones. But looking at the mountain of treats Dagesh has prepared for him, he could eat all week long and still not be through.

You've got to get your strength back up, Dagesh tells his friend. *We've got a long trip ahead of us.*

What do you mean? Mappiq says through a mouthful of food. He remembers how last year he had to run away when the field got flooded.

Do we have to move?

No, buddy, that's not what I mean, Dagesh grins. *We're going to fly into space!*

But we were already there, says Mappiq.

That's OK. We'll take a different route this time!

Three.

Two.

One.

GO.

Translated from the Czech by Alex Zucker

Illustrations by Axel Scheffler

The Day We Left Snogstrup

Dy Plambeck

Hey – my name's Agnes! I live on Poppy Road in the Bloomtown quarter of a small town called Snogstrup. It's so small that people often drive straight through it without even realizing that they've been here. Mikkel, Tobias and Lara live in the Bloomtown quarter too. All of the streets here are named after flowers, and the houses, gardens and hedges are almost identical. Mikkel lives on Eranthis Street, Tobias lives on Iris Street and Lara lives on Anemone Street. We're best friends. We've come up with lots of games together, like the Poo Game and Where Does the Priest Live?

I like the sound of midsummer. When we light the bonfire down by the village pond in Snogstrup and the fire crackles. When the evenings are bright, and Lara, Mikkel, Tobias and I play rounders on Anemone Street until bedtime. Plus, it's Mikkel's birthday at this time of year. His birthday is always a lot more fun than ours, because his Dad builds a chocolate-covered-marshmallow canon. We laugh so much that it's hard to catch them as they fly across the garden. We always end up covered in sticky marshmallow. Then Mikkel turns on the garden hose and the water fight begins!

* * *

For Mikkel's eleventh birthday, his dad hadn't built a chocolate-covered-marshmallow canon. Instead we sat in the garden eating cake with raspberry cream and drinking redcurrant juice. The breeze was warm. The leaves rustled. The treehouse in the large beech tree was slightly hidden behind branches and twigs. Mikkel has the best treehouse in the whole of Bloomtown. We can see all the way out over Snogstrup from the treehouse.

'Where's the chocolate-covered-marshmallow canon?' Tobias asked.

'I told my Dad not to build one this year,' Mikkel replied.

'BUT WHY?' I asked.

'It's for children,' Mikkel said.

He flicked through the pages of a book his mum and dad had given him for his birthday. It was all about an explorer who had scaled a mountain in Austria. There was silence around the birthday table. It was strange. Usually we spent the whole time talking over each other.

'Shall we play The Poo Game?' Lara asked all of a sudden.

'Yes!' I said.

The Poo Game is so much fun. We made it up ourselves. You have to run away and make sure you don't get hit by the dishcloth.

If it gets you, then you're the poo until you manage to throw it at someone else.

'No!' Mikkel said. 'I don't play games any more.'

Mikkel said that when you're eleven years old, you're not a child any more. That means you can't play. I thought that sounded odd. Tobias, Lara and I had all turned eleven. We still liked to play.

'So, what *do* you do, if you don't play any more?' I asked.

'You go exploring,' Mikkel replied.

Mikkel had read that the explorer in his book was eleven years old when he had climbed his first mountain. That was in the olden days. I don't really know when the olden days were, but they were a long time ago. My mum told me. She knows a lot of things. She told me that in the olden days, children didn't have time to be children. Instead, they had to go out picking turnips and chewing tobacco. People died really young too. They barely lived long enough to become grown-ups before kicking the bucket.

Mikkel wanted to go exploring. His mum told him he could sleep overnight in his treehouse as a special birthday treat. When his parents fell asleep tonight, he'd set off on his journey.

'If we went out exploring, we could see the sea every day,' Tobias said.

'And eat wild strawberries for supper,' Lara added.

'What will you discover on your journey?' Tobias asked.

'I won't know until I've discovered it,' Mikkel replied.

'How exciting! I want to come!' Lara said.

'Me too!' Tobias said.

All three of them looked at me.

Sometimes I feel a tear forming in the corner of my eye, right at the very edge. If I take a deep breath, the tear disappears back inside my body. If I don't, it tumbles over the edge and runs down my cheek. I looked at the cake. A raspberry had slipped out on one side. I took a deep breath. The tear disappeared back inside me. I didn't want to leave, but neither did I want to stay in Snogstrup without my best friends.

* * *

My mum and dad own the restaurant in Snogstrup. They love working. It's good to have a restaurant if you love to work, because it means you have to do exactly that all year round. Even at weekends. We've only ever been on holiday once. I was four years old. We went to Frankfurt in Germany. I can't remember anything about it apart from eating lasagne served in a little dish one evening at the hotel. Every other weekend, Lara goes away to stay with her dad, who lives in another town. Tobias left Ethiopia to come to Denmark when he was five months old, but it was so long ago that all he can remember is the smell of the red earth.

I never thought very much about the world outside of Snogstrup. I was sure that there was everything here that a girl could wish for. There was our school. Our church. Mum and dad's restaurant. Our village hall. Our treehouse in Mikkel's garden. There was the rubbish dump where we could go looking for things with Simon Scrapper. There was Harry the Hairdresser's salon. There was the village pond where we could catch tadpoles with our teacher, Karsten. There was Bicycle Betty's garden.

* * *

Mikkel left the birthday table that had been set up in the garden and ran into the house to fetch some paper and a pencil. He wrote a list of the things we'd need on our journey:

A knapsack to carry our things in
A sheath knife for whittling sticks
Matches to start fires with
A fishing net to catch food with
Food and water for the first few days

The mild breeze beneath the tree where we sat suddenly felt cold. I pulled my jumper tightly around me. My neck felt freezing. My hands were cold. It was just like that time I sucked on an icicle in the winter. It was strange, because even though I was cold, I started to sweat.

'We'll never find all of these things by this evening,' I said.

'Of course we will, it's no problem!' Mikkel said. 'Let's go see Bicycle Betty and Simon Scrapper.'

* * *

Just beside our school is the strangest house in Snogstrup, a crooked building with holes in the roof. Bicycles hang from the large apple trees in the garden. Bicycle wheels, saddles and rusty frames lie scattered across the front lawn. There is a proper sofa in the garden too, and the weeds are as tall as the flowers. Bicycle Betty and Simon Scrapper live here with their pig, Brian Hansen. I like Bicycle Betty a lot. Her eyes are as brown as chocolate ice cream. She has broad shoulders and strong arms, and she wears a boiler suit. Her hair is so curly and wild that birds could be nesting inside it.

When I saw Bicycle Betty in her garden fixing a pushbike, I felt another tear forming in the corner of my eye. I'd miss coming to her garden and having nettle soup when we left Snogstrup. I don't like missing anyone. My mum says it's good to miss people, because it means that we love them. At the bottom of Bicycle Betty's garden, there is a hole where grass snakes live. When I miss someone, it feels like I have a hole just like it inside my tummy.

'Bicycle Betty, we each need a knapsack!' Tobias said, as he made his way through the garden gate.

'Just like the one you had when you were a travelling craftsman,' Lara said to Simon Scrapper. He was sitting on the sofa in the garden. When Simon Scrapper was a travelling craftsman, he trekked all the way from Denmark to Turkey. He made his way from country to country working as a builder. Kind of like a nomad.

'I see! And what do you all need knapsacks for?' Simon Scrapper asked us.

We looked at each other.

'Uhhh…' Lara began.

'It's just for a game we're playing,' Mikkel said.

That made me feel so cross! Playing was exactly what Mikkel *didn't* want to do any more!

Bicycle Betty fetched her sewing machine. Simon Scrapper brought out a few rolls of fabric he'd found at the dump. We were allowed to choose our own fabric. Lara chose some with fir trees on it. Mine was multicoloured, like a rainbow. Bicycle Betty launched into action at her sewing machine. My knapsack looked so nice when it was done! It even had a little cord at one end that I could pull to close it. Suddenly I felt a little bit excited about our journey. Well, excited about packing my knapsack, at least.

Simon Scrapper came out of the house carrying a black, rectangular box. He handed it to Mikkel.

'It's a birthday present,' he said.

Mikkel opened the box. A sheath knife lay inside. It had a brown handle made of walnut. The blade of the knife gleamed in the light. It was beautiful! I think Mikkel liked it too, because his whole face turned red.

'Thank you!' he said.

'How did Simon Scrapper know that we needed a sheath knife?' Lara asked as we made our way out of the garden.

'I don't know,' Mikkel said.

Perhaps Simon Scrapper knew that we were planning a journey. When I turned around to look at him he was gazing out over the fields. I ran back into the garden and gave Bicycle Betty a big hug. She wrapped her strong arms around me.

* * *

Harry the Hairdresser was outside the front of his house trimming his garden hedge. He cuts and trims and prunes anything that he comes into contact with. His customers' hair. His trees. His lawn. He shaves off all of his own hair too. He's always carrying a pair of scissors. And he's always shouting, whether he's happy or cross.

'Where are you long-haired little ones off to?' he shouted, snipping at the air in front of him with his scissors. We ran straight past him. Harry the Hairdresser would probably be the only person in Snogstrup that I *wouldn't* miss when we left, I thought to myself. Although, perhaps I would miss him, even just a tiny bit. He was a lot of fun to tease. I liked to wave my long, dark curls in front of him. That always made him hot-tempered. Harry the Hairdresser hated long hair.

'Let's go down to the pond and see if Karsten is around,' Tobias said, 'he can probably get us a fishing net.'

* * *

As we made our way down to the village pond, I started thinking about what might be out there, beyond the fields on the outskirts of Snogstrup. Out in the big, wide world. There was probably a windmill. And a bus. When Lara's mum and dad got divorced, Bicycle Betty gave Lara a pair of binoculars. That way, she could look out towards her dad's house when she was with her mum in Snogstrup, and over to us in Snogstrup when she was with her dad. It was a clever idea! Lara had let me borrow her binoculars once. When I looked through them, I could see how big the world was. Even so, it was hard for me to imagine just how big it could really be. It must be bigger than the Snogstrup rubbish dump. That was the biggest place I knew.

Karsten was down at the pond catching tadpoles. Every spring, we spend our Natural Science classes catching tadpoles with him. In the winter, when there are no tadpoles to be caught, he sits behind his desk, sighing. When that happens, he tells us that all he can see are grey colours in the world. The houses are grey. The trees are grey. The children in his classroom are grey.

Karsten pulled a fishing net out of the pond. There were lots of tadpoles caught inside.

'Karsten, can we borrow a fishing net?' Lara asked him.

'Do you want to catch tadpoles?' Karsten asked us.

'Uh, no, we need to catch a ball that's stuck in a tree in my garden,' Mikkel said.

Karsten furrowed his brows.

'We can bring the net to school with us tomorrow,' Mikkel said.

I started to think about tomorrow. Tomorrow I wouldn't be in Snogstrup any more. I started to think about what Karsten would say when he saw all the unoccupied seats in our classroom. Perhaps he'd say: 'Now everything is grey again.' I felt empty inside when I thought about it. It felt a bit like when my mum and dad argue. My dad bangs the door and heads for the restaurant. Then it feels empty in the house, even though my mum and I are still there.

Karsten let us borrow one of his fishing nets. Now all we needed were matches and a little food and water.

'We can get food and water from your mum and dad at the restaurant,' Lara said.

* * *

My mum was lighting candles on the tables in the restaurant.

'Ask your mum if we can have some sandwiches,' Tobias said, giving me a nudge.

Slowly I walked towards her. Mikkel, Lara and Tobias followed me.

'Mum, we're hungry. Can we make some sandwiches?' I asked her.

'Hungry?' Mum repeated. 'Haven't you just been over at Mikkel's house eating birthday cake?'

'Yes, but it wasn't very nice,' Lara said.

'And there was no chocolate-covered-marshmallow canon!' Tobias added.

'No, because we're not children any more,' Mikkel interrupted.

'Oh, really? If you're not children, then what are you?' my mum asked.

We looked at each other. None of us could really answer the question.

'Well, we don't play any more, at any rate,' Mikkel replied.

'OK, then,' my mum said, 'then you'd best make yourselves some sandwiches.'

In the kitchen we made sandwiches with salami and cheese and took a bottle of water. Lara placed a box of matches on the table.

'Look what I found in the restaurant!'

Lara was so cheeky! She had just taken the matches without asking!

'We've got everything now!' Tobias said. His eyes shone.

'Come on, let's go home and pack our knapsacks!' Mikkel said.

My mum gave me a kiss on the cheek as we were setting off.

'I can't wait to pick elderflowers together tomorrow,' she said.

Every midsummer, my mum and I walk along the main road that runs through Snogstrup and pick elderflowers together. We press them and make cordial that my mum and dad sell in the restaurant. This time I couldn't hold back the tear that had appeared at the corner of my eye. It tumbled out and ran down my cheek. I walked behind Mikkel, Lara and Tobias on our way back to the Bloomtown quarter. I didn't want them to see I was crying.

* * *

That evening, I climbed up the little ladder to the treehouse in Mikkel's garden with my knapsack on my back. I had spent all evening sitting in my mum's lap.

'It's like you're my little girl again,' she said, hugging me.

Maybe Mikkel was right. Maybe I really wasn't a child any more. But if that was true, then I didn't know what I was. I thought about our journey. I didn't know what I was going to experience. It was hard. But then I remembered that I had my knapsack, made by Bicycle Betty. I had a sandwich from my mum and dad's restaurant. I had Karsten's fishing net. And I had my best friends, Tobias, Mikkel and Lara. Snogstrup would be with me, even after I'd left.

Lara, Mikkel and Tobias were already at the treehouse by the time I arrived. We looked out of the window. We could see the lights being turned off in Bicycle Betty and Simon Scrapper's living room. In my mum and dad's restaurant. In Harry the Hairdresser's salon. We didn't say a word to each other. Everyone felt sad and excited, I suppose.

'If we don't discover anything, we can always come home again,' Mikkel said, looking down at the ground.

He suggested that we rest for a little while. His parents stayed up very late at night watching the news on television. That's the kind of thing that parents like to do, sitting still and watching other people talk.

We crept into our sleeping bags. I closed my eyes. Perhaps I dreamt. Soon I was climbing down the ladder with Mikkel, Lara and Tobias. We made our way onto the main road that runs through Snogstrup. We carried on past the church and headed towards the restaurant. We turned round. My mum and dad were standing in front of the restaurant, waving at us. Bicycle Betty and Simon Scrapper were there too. And Karsten. And Harry the Hairdresser.

'Have a good trip!' they all shouted.

My body felt warm, just like it did when I sat by the midsummer bonfire at the village pond in Snogstrup. I started to smile. *Now* I could set off on our journey!

Translated from the Danish by Rosie Hedger

Illustrations by Charlotte Pardi

Why Rudolph Went to Rome Last Summer

Andri Antoniou

The day before our trip to Italy, last summer, you could find just about anything in my bedroom but standing space. My closet and drawers were open and their contents were lying on the floor.

'What's all this, Ioanna?' mum asked, rolling her eyes as she opened my bedroom door without even knocking. She stood inspecting the mess with her typical why-do-my-kids-always-bring-me-to-the-verge-of-a-nervous-breakdown expression.

'Don't worry. I've got it all under control,' I reassured her. 'I've watched several YouTube videos on how to pack like a pro. I know what I'm doing.'

She didn't seem convinced. 'By tomorrow morning, this suitcase,' I said and pointed at the yellow suitcase lying, still empty, on top of my bed, 'will contain everything a tourist needs to live her *dolce vita* in Rome.'

She still looked doubtful. 'Why won't you let me help you find the necessa…' she started, taking a few steps forward. But her right foot got tangled in the green Rudolph sweater that had been left by a heap of bikinis and she fell flat on the floor.

'Thank God your fall was softened and there weren't any injuries.' I pretended to laugh, praying she would find it funny.

Guess not. She got up, straightened her clothes and stroked her hair a few times. Some time ago she had read, in one of those magazines she calls 'my little moments of happiness', an article that said that every modern woman, with her hundreds of daily responsibilities, has to find her own way of controlling her nerves so that she won't explode all the time and have people mistakenly call her hysterical. Since then she's had the flattest hair in the house.

'You said you were old enough to pack your own suitcase,' she said when she was done with her relaxation exercises.

'*I am* old enough to pack my own suitcase. I'm going to middle school in the autumn, remember? I need trust. How else am I going to evolve into an independent, responsible individual?'

My arguments seemed to do the trick. She took a deep breath, then exhaled all the air through her mouth. Thankfully she left me alone with no further comment. It was around three o'clock in the afternoon. There was no reason whatsoever to get stressed that I might not manage to pack my suitcase in time. After all, it's a well-known fact that summer days are endless and hurrying can prove fatal.

And honestly I never understood how every time there is something that you *have* to do, instantly loads of other things appear that you *want* to do. Like for example paint your toenails coral-red, or chat online with that classmate who changed school, and country, and continent, three years ago, and now has so many stories from Japan to tell.

When I left my room for dinner, the clock said a few minutes past seven and my suitcase was as empty as my stomach.

'How's the packing going?' Dad asked as he brought the tray with the roast to the table.

'I'm one step away from closing it,' I said and stuffed a potato into my mouth so I wouldn't have to say any more.

'I want to pack my own suitcase, too,' Zoe interrupted. 'Why don't you ever let me pack my own suitcase? It's not fair! Not fair!' she screamed and banged her cutlery on the table.

Mum stroked her hair a few times and turned to look at Dad, who is bald and for whom this relaxation technique is not an option.

'What have we said about table manners, Zoe?' he asked.

Zoe pouted and put down her cutlery. 'Ioanna gets to do *everything* first,' she complained.

'In four years' time, when you're twelve, you have my word that you'll be free to pack your own suitcase. And I'm sure your older sister will be able to share her invaluable experience with you then,' Dad said, winking at me.

I'm not sure if the roast was a bit dry or if I was simply having trouble swallowing. I counted the hours left until my usual bedtime. A bit short of four hours. Absolutely no reason to stress. Four hours were more than enough. You could use them to pack your big yellow suitcase and *still* have time left to look for the most popular boards about Rome sights on Pinterest. Which was what I decided to do first.

It must have been while I was reading an article entitled 'The Ten Best Pizza Places in Rome' that my eyes fell on the time on the bottom-right corner of my screen. 11.48 p.m. How did my computer get its clock all wrong? I looked at my phone. 11.48. Was it really 11.48? When did it get to 11.48?

I jumped up from my chair more violently than someone who'd sat on a burning stove. I started throwing clothes, shoes and bags in every direction looking for things to take with me.

At some point my hand felt a notebook with a hard cover. The journal I kept in fourth grade! When was the last time I'd read it? I couldn't remember. I flicked through it absentmindedly, and my eyes fell on this line: *Dear Diary, today the headmistress slipped as she was coming into our classroom and her shoe fell off…*

I laughed. That really had been a funny day. The teacher had had to open one of the desk drawers and pretend to be looking for something so that the headmistress wouldn't see him laughing. Good times. I couldn't resist reading the next day's entry and the next and the next…

…And then we bought pizza from the best pizza place in Rome and we were devouring it in front of the Colosseum while a bulldog was barking its heart out…

I jumped up. What did I mean we were devouring pizza in front of the Colosseum while a bulldog was barking its heart out? Where on earth was I?

I looked around me. There was no Colosseum for miles. Only heaps and stacks of *things*. I looked at my phone. Oh, God.

It was already morning.

I had fallen asleep and, had it not been for the neighbours' bulldog barking, I wouldn't have woken up till Mum came barging into my room to ask if I'd finally managed to get ready.

OK, relax. Now was the time to prove I could rise to the occasion. Now was the time to stop my panic from leading me to do something rash. Now was the time to—

'Ioanna, are you ready?' I heard mum's voice in the corridor.

'Just a minute,' I shouted. 'I'm getting dressed.'

Too late now. Without wasting another second, I grabbed literally whatever I found in front of me and I shoved it in the suitcase. I was so stressed I could barely see what I was doing. Whatever didn't get stuffed into the suitcase I threw in the closet or kicked under the bed.

Fortunately I got lucky. Mum came into the room the exact moment I was closing my suitcase.

'I'm impressed,' was the first thing she said. 'Not only have you packed your suitcase but you've also managed to tidy your room! Well done, Ioanna. I must say I had my doubts.'

I don't know if I was imagining it or if at that moment I gulped a bit too noisily. 'I did tell you,' I mumbled, 'I had a… strategy.'

At the airport when we gave our suitcases to be weighted mine proved to be lighter than the rest.

'Did you pack everything?' Dad asked me.

'Just the essentials,' I smiled as convincingly as I could.

Mum looked at me discouragingly.

'It's important not to drag useless things on holidays.' I assured her. 'Honestly, all the experts say so.'

After take-off, the flight attendants came past with the carts and gave each passenger a tray with their food. I was racking my brains about whether I'd managed to include even *some* of the necessary things in my suitcase. Like for example a toothbrush. Or a few dresses. Or, umm, …

'Knickers!' I blurted out suddenly.

'Excuse me?' the stewardess looked startled. 'I… er… asked whether you want anything to drink.'

'Orange juice, please,' I said, and felt my cheeks turn bright-red.

My heart fluttered as we waited for our luggage. Time was passing and my suitcase was nowhere to be seen.

'I honestly won't be able to take it if Ioanna's suitcase is lost,' Mum muttered.

'What will she wear if her suitcase is lost?' Zoe asked.

That was a very good question. I should have already thought of alternatives. Because even if my suitcase hadn't been lost, the truth was I'd still probably need them. Maybe I could turn the bath towels or the sheets into dresses – I had watched enough DIY videos. People who took rags and a little later had transformed them into masterpieces – how hard could it be?

'Here's Ioanna's suitcase,' Dad said, and grabbed the suitcase from the carousel.

Worse luck.

As the taxi left the airport behind and entered the city, my mood got worse. Neither Rome's beauty, nor our walks around the city after we'd dropped our things at the hotel were enough to cheer me up.

'One, two, three… Say "*Bella Italia!*"' Dad said, as we posed in front of the Colosseum, but I barely managed to twist my lips.

Only the pizza that we had for lunch overlooking the Piazza di Spagna and the enormous ice cream for dessert managed to improve my mood a bit. But my mood plunged again in the afternoon when we found our way back to the hotel.

'It's ten past six,' mum checked her watch. 'You have about two hours to shower and change before we go out for tonight. And make sure I don't hear any fighting, understood?'

'Um… I'm thinking of wearing this again,' I mumbled. 'It's the most comfortable dress I have.'

Mum gave me a fierce look. 'You have got to be kidding,' she said. 'The whole day in the sun, you're soaked in sweat. Shower and get into some clean clothes right away.'

Zoe and I had our own room with a connecting door through to Mum and Dad's.

'Aren't you going to open your suitcase?' Zoe asked as she looked for something in hers.

'Of course I'll open my suitcase!' I said, my voice slightly higher-pitched than usual. 'After I'm rested.'

I waited for her to get in the shower, I took a deep breath and I opened it. What on earth? Of all my belongings in my room, how had I managed to bring this... mess? I was in big trouble if my parents saw it. What was I going to do now?

My eyes fell on Zoe's suitcase lying wide open. My hands were shaking as I searched through it. Mum surely would have packed her enough things to spend a month in Rome, not just five days. She surely wasn't going to need to wear towels or sheets. She had so many clothes that we could easily share them and still have some to spare. The only problem was that everything was too small. How was I going to fit?

'Put my things down!' I heard her scream, and turned.

'I... I was just... tidying them up,' I said.

'Muuum, Ioanna is messing with my stuff! Muuum, tell her!'

Mum appeared in our room within seconds.

'What did I just tell you? Didn't I say I didn't want any fighting?'

'What's the problem?' I shrugged. 'I just noticed that her suitcase was a mess and I was tidying it.'

'Then I'll tidy yours,' Zoe said and before I'd had time to stop her she'd opened my suitcase.

'No, don't...' I started, but it was too late.

Mum's jaw dropped to the floor. Once she'd seen the contents of my suitcase, she didn't even have the strength to stroke her hair.

'What is this, Ioanna?' she shrieked. 'Why on earth did you pack... *your pillow*?'

"No... I didn't... I mean...'

Mum kept digging and, a little later, lying on my bed was a small pile with the following objects: my pillow, a pink bathrobe, a pair of winter slippers shaped like chicken feet, one sock, my school backpack from last year with three books and two notebooks left in it, my left skate, a pair of jeans (hurray!), the blanket I snuggled in during the winter while I watched TV series on the computer, a pair of red wool leggings, two T-shirts (hurray!), four bikinis, my journal from fourth grade, three pairs of underwear (oh God, what bliss!) and the green sweater with Rudolph on it that I'd worn last Christmas.

"What's going on here?" Dad came in the room.

It didn't take long for him to understand what had happened. He took Mum by the hand and they went to their room to discuss my situation.

'You're stupid!' Zoe giggled. 'You have no idea how to pack a suitcase. Now you're going to have to wear chicken feet to learn your lesson!'

Fortunately Zoe was wrong. I didn't have to wear chicken feet. I did, however, have to wear red woollen leggings and a green Rudolph sweater. And all this on a summer night on the streets of one of the busiest cities in the world.

'You said it yourself,' Mum said, as we walked from our hotel to the Trevi Fountain. 'We have to help you evolve into an independent, responsible individual. And that clearly means you've got to learn to accept the consequences of your actions.'

As I was preparing to throw a coin into the most famous fountain in Rome, crowds of tourists had gathered around me and were looking at my outfit in wonder.

'It's the latest fashion,' I told them, but they didn't seem convinced.

'Ioanna, make a wish!' Dad shouted.

I didn't have to think about it too much.

'I wish to come back to Rome,' I whispered. 'But without Rudolph next time, OK?'

And I threw my coin in the fountain.

Translated from the Greek by Avgi Daferera

Illustrations by Lilian Brøgger

The Travel Agency

Maria Turtschaninoff

Hanna came in and closed the door behind her, setting off the piercing little entry bell overhead. Rain hammered against the window pane as she peeled off her sopping hood. She looked around and, for a second, wished she hadn't come. The travel agency was modern and starkly lit. Behind a curved counter of light-blue glass a receptionist with blonde hair in a neat ponytail was talking on a mobile phone. Hanna's trainers left dirty wet footprints on the polished stone floor. She was definitely out of place.

But she had run out of alternatives.

She picked up a brochure from a display stand and flipped through it. It was brand-new and glossy, filled with colourful illustrations. How was she supposed to find the right one?

The blonde receptionist tapped on her phone a few times, then put it down and looked at Hanna with a smile.

'Have you decided what you want?'

Hanna looked down at the brochure and opened a page at random.

'It's not easy. And these descriptions, I don't really get…'

The receptionist nodded understandingly. 'It can be confusing with so many options.' She scanned the empty office and adjusted the little blue scarf around her neck. 'We don't get many clients this early in the morning. If you like I can show you round and give you a bit more information. Maybe that will help you make up your mind.' She placed a small sign with the words 'Ring for assistance' next to a brass bell on the counter and walked over to a frosted glass door. She tapped in a passcode to open it and turned to Hanna.

'This way.'

Hanna adjusted the bag on her shoulder and followed silently behind the receptionist's clacking heels. She had learnt how to walk quietly that time she had to escape from the three sorcerers' dungeon maze on the island of Orlam.

They entered a long corridor with several doors, and large oil paintings hanging in heavy gold frames. The walls were the same dirty white-grey you find in hospital corridors and schools.

'This is our picture gallery,' said the receptionist, gesturing at the walls. 'Naturally, each picture is a portal. Some are very famous, others less so.'

Hanna saw pictures of ships on stormy seas, of mist-shrouded mountains and magnificent castles.

'Pictures are often the most accurate starting-off point for a journey. You get a clear image of your destination, which is not the case with other portals. That doesn't mean that you know exactly what awaits you once you step through, of course, but you have more of a chance to prepare yourself than you would with other portal passages. That's why picture passages belong to our deluxe range.'

'I don't have much money,' said Hanna quietly. She had emptied her bank account, withdrawn all of her birthday money and everything she had saved from her summer job the previous year, but she feared that the modest sum still wasn't enough. She looked carefully at every painting they passed. She liked some of them, especially the one of the ship, but there was nothing that she recognized.

'Then perhaps I might interest you in our small-object options. They tend to be a little more affordable. Not in the budget range of course; for that you can go to Tornado Tours.' The receptionist laughed when Hanna shook her head. 'No, I understand. Why anybody would voluntarily travel by tornado in this day and age is beyond me!' She opened a door.

'In here we have the small portals.'

Hanna stepped into a white room filled with brightly illuminated glass display cases. Inside them, laid out on black velvet, was an assortment of items: rings of various metals, a knife, a pair of shiny red shoes, several books, an amulet that consisted of two snakes biting each other's tails and a variety of keys.

'Some keys will always open to the same destination regardless of what door you enter through,' explained the receptionist, leading Hanna to the display cases. 'Perhaps you read about that in the brochure?' Hanna passed the brochure, now damp and crumpled, from one hand to the other. 'While other keys are more sensitive and require a specific door, or point in time, or person to turn them. Of course, we have employed such individuals as door openers, and you will find the schedule for the time-specific keys in the brochure. Over here we have the door gallery.'

Hanna looked at each key carefully. There were big ones and small ones, some shiny-new and some that looked several hundred years old. But none of them felt right. Neither did the knife, nor the red shoes.

'Are you travelling alone?'

Hanna took a step back from the display cases. What if she had to bring a grown-up along? She grimaced to herself.

'It's easiest to travel alone, you see. Certain portals only accept one traveller at a time. Have you considered our travel insurance? It doesn't cover everything, of course. Dragon capture falls outside the policy, and no one covers acts of gods these days.' She laughed.

'No, I haven't...' Hanna looked down at the floor, disappointed. None of these objects stood out to her. None of them inspired the same giddy sense of wonder as she had felt when, one day in early spring, she had walked through the entrance to Grandma's pergola and suddenly found herself somewhere else entirely. In a place where everything was vibrant and fantastical.

She had made a friend there, in the other world, where the woods smelt like dark chocolate and the trees spun spells and weaved dreams between their branches. A friend the likes of which she had never had here, in this world of loneliness and rain and school and stinky sports halls. *Sannala*. Hanna held the name close to her heart like a glowing ember. The memory of Sannala was the only thing that kept Hanna warm through her cold everyday life. Sannala with her blue hair and skin like streaked granite. Sannala who could talk to birds and who dived headlong into every new adventure with a hearty chuckle. And there, in the island realm, Hanna had been a different person too – she was strong; she was admired. Together she and Sannala fought against sorcerers and monsters; they liberated the fairy queen Malkian's enchanted ring from the cloud city and let the lonesome tree of sorrow sing once more, for the first time in seven hundred years. And when the sea witch attacked the island realm and made the sea impassable, Queen Malkian entrusted them with the quest to save her queendom. The inhabitants were starving to death. They relied on fish, because the islands barely grew anything good to eat. The witch kept them from sailing away to trade the pollen of the silverbloom, which grew so abundantly on the islands' green mountain slopes, for food and healing potions.

Sannala and Hanna stripped off their clothes on the Golden Cape shores, where the hot sand smelt like toffee and burnt sugar. They hung their swords, won in defeat of the volcano demon Jor, around their waists. They waded, hand in hand, out into the warm turquoise sea to confront the witch face to face. As soon as they set foot in the water, a wild raging wave surged towards them, with the cruel eyes of the sea witch blazing out from its yellow foam.

When they dived in they were forced to let go of each other's hands.

Everything became a blur of bubbles and flurries. Hanna was tossed to and fro, until she didn't know which way was up or down, and had to fight her way to the surface for air.

When she re-emerged she found herself no longer in the turquoise sea but in a cold grey sea bordered by smooth rocks. And she was alone…

'Will you be taking much luggage?' The receptionist's voice interrupted her thoughts. 'One piece of hand luggage per person is included in the price of most journeys, but anything more costs extra. Usually the price is determined by weight, though to some destinations, such as those accessible via bodies of water—'

'I only have this bag.'

'Good. Sensible, too, travelling light. People rarely need everything they imagine to be essential.' The blonde woman led Hanna back out into the corridor and to another door.

'Here we have the larger passage portals.' She opened the door. 'Wardrobes, mirrors, bags…'

Hanna stepped inside. This room looked different from the boring white rooms they had previously seen. The walls were decorated in a wallpaper of tree branches covered with apple-blossom buds. To Hanna's left there was an old fireplace that looked as though it had been out of use for at least fifty years, and from the ceiling there hung a chandelier draped in a white cloth that filled the room with a warm filtered light. A large dark wooden wardrobe stood against the far wall, flanked by two oak doors, so old and polished they might have been made of stone. They had neither keyhole nor handle. In front of the fireplace was a sunken leather armchair and several old suitcases. On the right-hand wall there hung a series of full-length mirrors with silver, gold and carved wooden frames.

'We haven't had a chance to renovate this room yet,' said the receptionist apologetically. 'This used to be a residential building, built by the merchant Noel Kit – ever heard of him? Our owner, Alice Silwe, bought the entire estate just last year. Many of the portals you have seen today came from Kit's collections. We suspect that the fireplace might also be a portal, so this room shouldn't be disturbed before it's investigated fully.'

Hanna immediately walked over to the fireplace, but it was cold and mute and didn't speak to her at all. She stared disappointedly into the black space. How would she ever find a way back?

'The, um, the brochure mentions other portals as well? Woods, lakes, a cloud you can fly on, a star you can fly to—'

'Our outdoor portals.' The receptionist nodded. 'Classics. The woods are among the oldest known portals. As are holes in the ground you can crawl through or fall down. Seas and lakes are very steady—'

'Is there an age limit?'

Hanna barely dared ask. She was so afraid of the answer. Despite numerous attempts, the entrance to the pergola had never led to another world again. Only to a withering lilac bush. She had tried to dive back into that cold sea and return to Sannala and the Golden Cape, until the salty water filled her nostrils and forced her to surface, coughing, her throat burning. She had clambered up on the rocks, slippery with slimy green seaweed, and wept. Sannala would think she had drowned. Or that the sea witch had taken her. Maybe she had tried to barter with her own life in exchange for Hanna's and the witch had tricked her! Or, even worse, maybe she thought that Hanna had betrayed her. Abandoned her.

One spring and one summer had passed since then. Hanna had had a birthday in that time. What if she was too old? Grown-ups couldn't travel between the worlds as easily as children.

'Ah!' the receptionist lit up. 'Good question! It is true that spontaneous travellers have almost always been children. Some portals, like that wardrobe,' she pointed, 'only work for children, unfortunately. The same goes for holes in the ground. Experience has shown that young adults can also pass through the more well-known, reliable portals. Though I'm afraid it is often the case that the ability to cross over decreases with each passing year.' She looked kindly at Hanna. 'But you are still young. Then, when it comes to the return journey—'

Hanna interrupted her suddenly. 'What about time?'

'Time?' As the receptionist looked at her, Hanna thought that her eyes saw too much. She turned around and examined the fireplace again. The wallpaper to the right of it showed apple blossoms in full bloom. Weren't they buds just a moment ago?

'Yes, time is often different, isn't it? There and here.' Hanna swallowed.

'It's true. Many portals are temporally volatile. That is why we ask for payment in full prior to departure.'

A bird was sitting on one of the branches. It was turquoise, as turquoise as that sea had been, back there, in the place she wanted to return to more than anything. She thought she could almost hear the bird singing.

'I heard,' she said in a small voice, 'that time goes much faster in the other worlds than it does here. That one day here can be a hundred years there.' In which case there would be no Sannala any more. Hanna could hardly bear to think of it.

'Sometimes.' Hanna heard sympathy in the woman's voice. She didn't want sympathy. She wanted to go back. She wanted to go home.

'But not always. Sometimes time moves faster here than it does there. It varies greatly, and no one has been able to figure out what governs it all. Our owner, Alice, is convinced that it depends on the traveller.'

A glimmer of water shone beneath the apple blossoms. Hanna caught the scent of toffee and burnt sugar. Someone was walking on the shore and gazing out across the turquoise sea. Someone with tangled blue hair.

She turned to the receptionist.

'Well, thank you for the tour.'

The woman was taken aback, but quickly hid her surprise. 'So do you have a specific destination in mind? We have an app that matches destinations to portals. It's still in the beta phase, but you can install it on your phone and—'

'No, thanks.' She walked hastily out of the room. Her heart was racing, pounding. She had no time to lose. The receptionist followed after her, down the corridor and back to the frosted-glass door. A few clients were visible out in the waiting room. Just when the blonde woman was about to unlock the door she stopped. Hanna held her breath.

'Your bag! You left it behind.'

'Oh, I'm sorry, I'll run and get it. I'll just be a second. You have clients waiting,' Hanna pointed, 'I'll knock when I'm back.'

'It's OK, I'll wait, but do hurry.'

Hanna ran down the corridor and into the room with the fireplace without making a sound. The receptionist stuck her head round the door to the waiting room. 'I do apologize about the wait – I'll be with you in just a moment.' She closed the door again and followed slowly after Hanna.

When she came back into the room, it was empty. Hanna and her bag were nowhere to be seen. There was a strong smell of burnt sugar. The receptionist checked the wardrobe: it was locked. The doors were closed and hostile. She examined the mirrors, ran her fingers along the glass and frames, then shook her head. Finally she came over to the fireplace. The smell became more intense. She peered into the fireplace and then at the wall next to it. The wallpaper showed a wild blooming forest filled with blue-green birds. Through the branches she caught sight of a golden beach where two figures were embracing.

She took her mobile phone out from her pocket at once and dialled a number.

'Hi. She found a portal. No, it wasn't the fireplace. The wallpaper. It must date back to when the house was built. Of course, I'll make sure it is secured.'

She listened carefully. Then smiled widely.

'That's good to hear. Then she should have plenty of time to put things right. No, I don't think we should expect her return.'

She smiled, humbled. 'Thank you, Alice, that's very kind. And I'd just like to say that I think it is a wonderful thing you are doing. Helping the ones who... Yes, yes. I know.'

And she hung up, without saying goodbye.

Translated from the Swedish by A.A. Prime

Illustrations by Kamila Slocinska

The Honey-Bee Cemetery

Stefan Bachmann

Benny moved into Hawksdale on a whispery, bleak autumn day. No one met him at the station, so he dragged his suitcase behind him up the long, long driveway, bumping it over the gravel.

'It used to be a prison,' Aunt Lucette said, when she opened the front door. She glanced worriedly down at him, at his banged-up suitcase and his clothes, which were not new. Benny glanced back at her, equally worried. He wasn't sure why she had told him that, whether it had been meant as a selling point or a deterrent. He felt like an odd sort of beetle, invading her lovely, violet-smelling hallway.

'I hear you don't speak?' Aunt Lucette said, walking ahead into the house. They passed through a parlour, a dining room, a library, until they came to the back parts of the house with its narrow rooms and dusty skirting boards. She wrung her hands – bird-bone thin and waxy-skinned. 'Not since the accident.'

Benny nodded, but he was walking behind her and she didn't see. She half-turned and frowned at him.

Aunt Lucette was his father's sister. She had never liked Benny's mum. Aunt Lucette had two children named William and Carlisle, fishy-smelling twins, a year or two older than Benny. Then there was Uncle Marlow somewhere, but all Benny remembered of him was that he was jowly and red-faced and had begun shouting once at a Christmas party and been thrown out into the rain.

'This will do, won't it?' Aunt Lucette said, showing him through a doorway. 'Most of the big rooms are locked, I'm afraid. Heating costs. And the garden is off-limits too. I'll just expect you to occupy yourself until the term starts, all right? I'm… very sorry about your mother.'

She left quickly, tossing one more anxious glance over her shoulder, and closed the door behind her. Benny set down his suitcase and slumped on the edge of the bed, wishing he could be anywhere else and knowing that wishing things made no difference at all.

* * *

Hawksdale was a big house, powder-white-and-pink on the inside, mouldering and crumbling from the outside, and almost entirely covered in ivy. Great, dark pines stood behind it, beyond the high stone wall of the gardens.

'How d'you like your room?' Carlisle shouted, poking his head round the door. 'Mum didn't want you in the good guestrooms.

She locked them all up with the skeleton key right before you got here.'

'Yes,' said his brother, poking his head in too. 'Because you're not really a guest. More like a good deed we've got to feed three times a day.'

'William!' Aunt Lucette screeched from somewhere down the hall, but Benny just turned away. He found it difficult to care these days: about moving, about Aunt Lucette's curious glances, about his cousins. And because he didn't care, his cousins soon tired of him and went away.

His room was small and bare. It had one window and an iron bedstead, painted with chipped whitewash. A small, terrifically ancient-looking cupboard hung on the wall. He ignored it at first, but later, while he was unpacking, he peered inside. There wasn't anything in it except cobwebs. Benny closed it again, and he wasn't sure why he had bothered looking.

All day, he lay on his bed, listening to the twins shouting outside on the lawn. Sometimes Aunt Lucette's sharp heels went clacking through the silence of the house, from parlour to kitchen to an upstairs bedroom, like a soldier patrolling his beat. It was her house, the heels said, as they cut the space into jagged pieces – her house.

At some point, a car engine turned off in the driveway. The front door slammed. An hour passed, and Benny imagined they must be eating dinner. They hadn't called him, but he wasn't hungry anyway.

* * *

He woke up in the middle of the night to a sound. At first he was sure he was listening to his cousins murmuring in the corridors,

165

perhaps playing a prank. But this sound was far too close. When he listened closely it sounded like voices, very close by.

Benny got up slowly and moved towards the wall. The window was closed. There was nothing else in the room but that old cupboard. Was the sound coming from *inside*?

His heart leapt a little. What if it was a rat? Or worse, spiders? Benny hated spiders. But spiders didn't make noise, did they? Only the things they caught made noise, and then only for a bit.

Benny opened the cupboard in a burst and leapt backwards, just in case. He gasped. The cupboard – which this morning had still had a solid wooden back – now looked into another room. More of a shed, really, cramped and dirty. The floor was covered in straw. A bucket stood in one corner. And there were three women in great dresses and aprons and yellowed caps, sitting against the far wall. All three looked up when he opened the cupboard. Benny slammed the little door shut and pressed his back to it, eyes wide.

What on earth?… A bit of light still leaked from around the edge of the cupboard door. He could hear the women beyond, muttering to each other, their skirts skittering over straw.

This wasn't possible. There *was* no room on the other side of that wall. Right next to the cupboard was a window, and that window looked out onto a clearing, a hose coiled in the grass like an old dead snake and the dark pine brooding overhead. Just to be sure, Benny hurried to the window, opened it carefully and looked along the wall. There was no shed, no light.

He went back to the cupboard and opened it very slowly, so that the hinges wouldn't squeak.

There was the room again. One of the women had left. In fact, it looked as if some time had passed, though the door had only

been closed for a moment. There were only two women now, one very old, one young and pointy-faced, with wild black hair. The older woman seemed terribly worried. She was tangling her greasy, dirty fingers together and rocking back and forth. But the girl sat sharp-chinned and proud, staring straight ahead with a vicious sort of fury.

'Stupid Lord Hawksdale,' she hissed. 'Stupid mistress. Stupid everyone in that house.'

'Shush! Shush, Hezra!' the older woman cried, her voice high and trembling. 'You'll make it worse if they hear you.'

The girl snorted and looked away. Benny stood at the cupboard, uncertain what to do. And all at once, the girl looked up and stared at Benny with such glittering intensity that he gasped.

The girl didn't move. Just watched him, frozen, like a wild animal. At some point the older woman seemed to fall asleep.

Benny let his breath out, so, so slowly, his heart hammering in his ears. The girl couldn't see him, could she? This had to be a dream. But she was still staring at him, her eyes like bright marbles in her thin, dirty face.

Benny's foot nudged a splinter in the floorboards. He ducked down to pull it out. When he brought his face back up to the cupboard, the girl was gone. Benny squinted into the dark. And then her face appeared at the back of the cupboard, startlingly close, and Benny almost screamed.

'Hello, ghost,' she said, and looked at him coolly, her gaze hooded.

Benny stood very still.

'Don't you speak?' she asked. 'Aren't you supposed to deliver some great wisdom and then help me out of this scrape?'

Benny shook his head.

'Ah,' she said. 'You're not an angel, then.'

He shook his head again, emphatically.

'You *are* a bit short for an angel,' she said. And then she looked quickly back over her shoulder at the sleeping woman. 'I asked for something to come help me. That's why I thought you were maybe an angel. They're going to hang me the day after tomorrow.'

Benny's eyes widened.

The girl tossed up her hands in annoyance. 'I knew it was a mistake coming to the big house. Everyone at St Francis's, they said, you mustn't go. You're too naughty and strange, you'll get in trouble. But I got in trouble there in the workhouse too, and the food's awful, so I thought it would be better getting in trouble here. Well, it wasn't.'

Benny stared at her, waiting for more. She only frowned at him sidelong.

He cleared his throat. 'Wh...' he began. 'Why are they going to hang you?' It came out in a croak. He hadn't heard his voice in so long, and it frightened him a little, all those words floating in the air where anything could come of them. He half-wished he could snatch them back, but at the same time he desperately wanted to know the answer to his question.

'You do speak!' the girl exclaimed. 'Why the hanging? They said it was me that made all the bees die in Lord Hawksdale's hives. But it wasn't. I only buried a few. Laid each one in the dirt behind the house, with a pine cone for a funeral wreath. But they thought it was witchcraft, done for a spell.' The girl gave Benny a keen look. 'Do I look like a witch to you?' she demanded, and Benny shook his head.

'The others they got for witchcraft too,' the girl said. 'Three workmen, four maids and the housekeeper. Soured milk, broken eggs, boils, it's all our fault. Whenever Lord Hawksdale gets into some sort of trouble, it's always best to distract with a witch-hunt.' She looked away bitterly.

'What are you doing in the big house?' she asked. Her face darkened. 'Are you the Lord's son?'

'No,' said Benny. 'I'm nobody's son.'

She nodded. 'I'm nobody's daughter. Why wouldn't you talk at first?'

'Because,' said Benny. 'I suppose I didn't see the point.'

'Ghost?' she whispered. 'Ghost, d'you think I can escape this place?'

'I'm not sure,' said Benny.

'I bet I could,' she said, and she pressed close to the cupboard, and she no longer looked haughty, but desperate and alive. 'You could give me the key.'

'What key?'

'The big key, the one that opens all the doors. Lord Hawksdale carries it everywhere.'

'There is no Lord Hawksdale any more,' said Benny. 'It's just my aunt and uncle now, and my cousins, and... Aunt'd never give me the key. She doesn't want me here.'

'You could steal it,' said Hezra. 'Please, they'll never guess. I don't want to be hanged.'

Benny bit his lip. There was a commotion behind Hezra, at the shed's door. Three men burst in, wearing swords and jerkins with the crest of a hawk. The tallest had some sort of document in his hands. The older woman began to scream, and Hezra slammed the cupboard door in Benny's face.

* * *

Benny read wildly the next day, stealing books from the down-stairs library and dashing back to his room, quick as a shadow. There were so few things about Hawksdale; it was not an important estate in the scheme of things. A country manor from the fifteenth century. A low-security prison for pickpockets and swindlers in the nineteenth. Given up to private ownership due to rising maintenance costs in 1986. There was nothing at all about a witch trial, or Hezra, or dying bees.

Not that it mattered. He didn't have much time. He couldn't see anything through the cupboard by day, but as soon as he had dared reopen it the night before, the older woman had been gone. Hezra was curled up in the corner, staring into nothing. She had been found guilty of consorting with evil spirits, bewitching the honey bees and burying them in the earth for reasons unknown.

'I'll run away,' she told him, when he said he'd get the key. 'If I can get out, I'll run all the way to Cotton Hill, three towns over or more. I'll get work there. They'll never find me, nor see me again.'

Benny nodded and they'd sat together, one on either side of the cupboard, murmuring all through the night.

* * *

That afternoon, Benny went slowly to his Aunt's study and knocked at the door. She opened it and smiled down at him, her rabbit eyes watery.

He stared at her, his heart beating very fast.

'Yes, Benny?' she said.

'I… ' he began, slowly and quietly. 'I think there's a bird in the chimney downstairs. If it comes through it'll get soot all over everything—'

Aunt Lucette let out a shriek and pushed past him. He watched her go. Then he crept into her study. He found the greatest, rustiest key he had ever seen, lying half-hidden under some papers on her desk. He snatched it up and ran.

* * *

The moment the sun had set, he opened the cupboard door. Hezra was sitting against the far wall. She held a honey bee in her hand, and cried over it bitterly.

'I've got it,' Benny whispered. 'I stole the key!'

She looked up and wiped her nose on her sleeve. Benny held up the great old key, and Hezra, creeping over the floor and rising, looked at him through the open cupboard. They were face-to-face, six centuries apart. Benny smiled at her quickly. She smiled back. He handed her the key. She hesitated, and then passed him her honey bee, brittle and delicate as a dried flower.

'Why'd you bury the honey bees?' he asked, just as she was about to close the door.

'I don't know,' she said. 'To remember them, I suppose. No one even noticed they were dying. No one cares for us either, d'you see, Ghost? But it won't stop us. The bees only go a little ways in their life. They're dead in three winters. But they're ever so busy while they're alive. It's like they don't even know. Or they do, and they don't mind.'

Benny felt very cold. 'I hope you get away,' he said. 'I hope… I hope you'll be happy.'

There was a sound beyond the wooden walls of the shack, out in another yard, in another time: the sound of footfalls and loud voices.

'Hurry,' Benny said. 'Run.'

'I'll be all right,' said Hezra. 'You will be too.'

She closed the cupboard quickly. Benny went to bed and blocked his ears.

* * *

The next morning, he opened the door and looked in. There was no room beyond. Only the pitted wooden back of the old cupboard and the knobbly skeleton key placed neatly on the shelf, like an invitation.

He stared at it a while, thinking all kinds of thoughts, like whether he was mad, or whether Hezra had escaped. In the end, Benny closed the cupboard and put on his boots and went outside.

He walked around the house, breathing in the crisp morning air. He unlocked the door in the garden wall and walked beneath the trees of the honey-bee cemetery, now so tall and wild, surrounding the house and its inhabitants, aloof and older than all of them put together. The grass was wet and bright with dew. It would be turning to frost soon, as autumn ended, but now the sun was out. Everywhere the bees were buzzing.

Illustrations by Philip Waechter

Between the Trees

Katherine Woodfine

She'd been riding since dawn. She'd always prided herself on being a good rider, but now she felt no pride, only exhaustion. It was all she could do to slide, awkwardly and painfully, from the pony's back.

Her legs felt weak, as though they might collapse underneath her. Hobbling, she tethered Brownie to a low-lying mossy branch and then stood back, breathing in gulps of air. It was scented richly of earth and leaves: a forest smell.

The clearing was a small one, the trees densely crowded, blocking out what little was left of the light. The ground was covered with a rough mess of dry leaves, twisting roots and pine needles. Twigs cracked underfoot and a bird fluted one long, low note, high up in the trees.

She eased herself down wearily onto a clump of roots. Was this the right place to stop for the night? Was it too exposed, too close to the road, too damp, too *something else* that she didn't even know she was supposed to beware of? For the hundredth time that day, she wished she knew more of the woods. But she was a young lady – not a forester. This was not the place that she belonged.

Of course, she'd ridden through woods like this a dozen times before, but it had been different then. Then, she'd been wearing her thick, warm, newly laundered riding habit; her polished boots; her hat with its cockade of pheasant feathers. Then she'd been laughing over her shoulder to Edward, relishing the wildness of the woods, the rush of the wind in the trees, knowing that a good dinner would be waiting for them at home. A hot bath, the fire crackling in the hearth, a steaming bowl of Agnes's soup on the table, or stew with good brown gravy. Bread warm from the oven. Climbing into her bed between fresh linen sheets.

All that was gone now. No fire, no bowl. No soft, warm bed. Home was far away, and Edward was still farther. No fresh linen sheets for him, only the muddy battlefield of Naseby. But she wouldn't think about that now; she couldn't. Better to think of how it felt to be here, cold and alone in the woods at nightfall. Better to think of her hands, sore and blistered from gripping the reins all day; of the hungry ache in her stomach.

Much better to think of that than of leaving the house that morning. The frantic scramble of hooves clattering in the yard; the rattle of a sabre; Agnes weeping in the kitchen; her own breaths, hard and sharp; and her father's voice: '*Go!*'

There had been no time then to think about what she was leaving behind her. She'd had to go exactly as she was, in the ordinary gown she'd been wearing that morning. Agnes had pushed the old green cloak into her hands; now Isabella drew it more closely around her shoulders. It smelt of home, and although she knew it was silly, she felt somehow as though it had the power to keep her safe. Drawing the hood over her head made her feel invisible – even to Cromwell's men, out there somewhere, on the road.

In the treetops there was a sudden rustle of leaves, a clamour in the dark. For a moment she stiffened and clutched at the paper tucked safely inside the bodice of her gown, but it was nothing but a bird, and she let out a long, ragged breath of relief.

She'd seen them only once that day, but that had been more than enough. A party of men on tall black horses, riding hard. They wore iron skullcaps and pistols at their sides; and their clothes were black too. She had thought of a flock of ravens, sweeping across a winter sky.

'*Go*, Isabella!' she'd heard her father say.

And so she had gone, spurring the pony onwards, away from the road, along a twisting track between the trees that led into the heart of the forest. She'd been going for miles; now, at dusk, she was no longer entirely sure where she was.

She dropped her head into her hands. She ought to be called Mary or Liza, she thought, and to wear a neat brown dress and a little white cap. A Mary or a Liza would be sensible and practical. They wouldn't giggle at prayers or daydream at their lessons. They would know how to do this: how to find their way, how to take care of themselves in the woods. How to build a fire and prepare food, and stay safe from Cromwell's men.

But she was no Mary or Liza. She was Isabella. Ribbons in her hair. Hands as soft as butter. She couldn't remember the last time she'd made her own bed or unlaced her own gown. 'Spoilt little madam,' Agnes used to say when she was vexed. Now she felt a sudden longing for Agnes to be there, stroking her hair and singing a lullaby. She wanted to make herself small, to bury her head into Father's shoulder until the world disappeared. But she was a little girl no longer. She was here – alone in the woods – and it was growing dark.

As if he knew what she was thinking, Brownie snuffed a hot, hay-scented breath of air against her ear. He seemed contented enough, stooping to nibble gently at a patch of grass. She put out a hand to touch his warm, velvet-soft neck, and it steadied her. She felt able to push herself upwards onto her feet again, grabbing a handful of ferns to rub the perspiration from the pony's sides.

She *had* to do this. Father was counting on her. 'I know you can do it. You can ride as fast as any of the men. Go now and ride hard to your uncle's house in the city of York – and put this message into your uncle's hand and no other.' She had wept and argued; she had not been able to bear the thought of leaving him. Everyone said the Parliamentarian troops were approaching. Everyone said they would burn the house of any Malignant to the ground lest he be hiding the escaped King. Who knew what they would do to one so loyal to King Charles as her father, whose only son had carried arms for His Majesty until the day he fell on the fields of Naseby? She'd begged to stay and help, but Father had been more determined than she had ever seen him. '*This* is the best way for you to help me. You are the only one I can trust. Isabella, you *must* go.'

She must. She must be brave; she must deliver her father's letter. But she would not be able to find her way through the woods at night, so for now she must make camp here. She must look after Brownie and feed herself and try to rest, for there would be another hard day's riding tomorrow.

A fire then, first of all. She knew that she should start with stones, and she stumbled about the clearing in search of them. They felt heavy and damp and cold in her chilly hands, as she arranged them in a wobbly circle on a patch of bare ground. Next came the sticks: strong, stout ones; little twigs to make her kindling; and some pieces of dried-out bark. Thank goodness that Agnes had put the tinderbox into the saddlebag. Her hands shook as she struggled to drop a spark onto the tinder and make a flame.

But it lit at last, and she sat back on her heels and stared at the tiny orange flame as it began to lick at the edges of the bark and to burn the twigs with a warm crackling sound. She felt a glow of triumph, as she stretched out her cold hands to the flickering flames. She had done it – she had made a fire! Perhaps she could do this after all.

But she must think of food next, for she could no longer ignore the gnawing growl in her stomach. The hunk of bread and cheese from the kitchen had been eaten long ago on the road. Now she must deal with the rabbit.

She swallowed and opened the saddlebag. The rabbit had been a gift from the old poacher, kindly meant. A gesture of thanks for all the times that her father had looked the other way and let him take fish from his streams and rabbits like this one from his woods. Now she let it flop out onto the ground before her – glassy-eyed and dead. She put out one finger and touched its fur. It still felt soft.

She knew a rabbit had to be skinned and cleaned; then she could roast it over the fire. But how? Mary or Liza – they would have known. But to Isabella a rabbit was a pretty creature nibbling grass in a meadow; a rabbit-fur collar on a new winter gown. She shuddered at the thought of what she must do.

Agnes would have shaken her head at her. 'Daft lass,' she would have said. Agnes would have rolled up her sleeves and got on with the work, and now she, Isabella, must do the same. She had to eat, and the rabbit was all she had. She had a knife – and surely it could not possibly be so very difficult to skin a rabbit?

She set her jaw and forced herself to pick up the limp, drooping body. Where ought she to begin? The head – or the feet? The feet would be easiest: the thought of slicing the rabbit's neck made her feel ill. But would it be the proper thing to take off its head first? She knelt on the ground and laid the rabbit flat before her, and sucked in a deep breath. Then, before she could change her mind, she pushed the knife against its throat. She felt flesh tearing and the brittle crunch of bone. She pushed harder, a sob rising in her throat.

'You're making a mess,' said a voice.

Isabella jumped and dropped the knife; it skittered away from her, rattling against the stones.

The voice seemed to have spoken out of nowhere. It was as though one of the trees had suddenly begun to talk.

'Wh-who's there?' she demanded, her hand shooting out to recover the knife.

'Don't fret,' said the voice, sounding almost amused now – and a moment later, a girl stepped out from between the trees.

She was younger than Isabella – and shorter and sturdier. She had brown hair and a rough brown cloak, like something a boy would wear. 'I'll not hurt you. But I reckon you could do with some help.'

The girl knelt down beside her and picked up the rabbit. Her movements were soft but sure, like a bird's. She did not touch the knife, but took the rabbit by one foot and pulled it apart with some quick, mysterious gesture. A moment later, she had slipped her fingers right underneath the skin, and was peeling it deftly away, as easily as if she were pulling a glove off her own hand.

'Then you cut the neck like this – see?'

She picked up the knife and it was done in one swift, neat stroke.

'How did you do that?'

The girl slit open the rabbit's belly with a gentle movement of the knife, reached inside and pulled out something – its innards, Isabella thought with a shudder – before tossing it aside and wiping her fingers casually on her cloak. 'It's not hard. I can show you, if you like – and how to cook it too. That's if you'll share your supper with me.'

Half an hour later, they sat side by side in silence, sucking rabbit's meat from the bones. Isabella thought she had never tasted

anything so delicious in all her life. She let out a long, slow breath: for the first time since she had left the house that morning, she felt almost calm.

'The likes of you shouldn't be out here in the forest, alone,' observed the strange girl at last.

Isabella felt indignant. Perhaps she did not know how to skin a rabbit, but she had ridden hard all day, and now here she was, sitting on the ground, eating the rabbit they had roasted together, over the fire that she had built. Besides, this girl was younger than she was, and no more than a poor peasant. What right had she to tell her what she should and should not do? 'Why shouldn't I? You are,' she declared.

'That's different. I've nowhere else to go.' The girl chuckled. 'Besides, I can get the skin off a rabbit without crying like a newborn babe.'

Isabella stared at her. Her mouth opened to fling out a haughty retort, but her own curiosity got the better of her. 'What do you mean, you've nowhere else to go? Where's your home?'

'Not got one.'

'But you must have come from *somewhere*?'

'Well, I did have one. But it's gone.'

'How? Why?'

The girl sighed and tossed a rabbit bone aside. 'I can see you're a one for questions. I lived with my mam. She was a cunning woman. She helped folk – when they were with child or if they were ill. But then the men came and took her. They said she was a witch – and they burned her.'

Isabella gasped. 'How terrible!'

The girl's face was expressionless. Her eyes were grey as stone, pale like lichen on the bark of a tree. 'It was a warning, they said.'

'What will you do now?'

'I dunno. But I couldn't stay. Mam told me I had to run – as far away as I could, else the ravens would take me too.'

'The ravens?' Isabella stared at her. 'Do you mean Cromwell's men? The Parliamentary troops?'

The girl shrugged. 'King's men, Parliament's… they're all the same to me. Just as bad as each other.' She spat solemnly on the ground.

'That's not true! The King's men are fighting for what's good and right and honourable! They wouldn't do something like that.'

The girl just snorted. 'That's not what I've heard.'

'My father is loyal to the King! And my brother is too – or he was…'

'*Was?*' It was the strange girl's turn to ask a question.

'He fell in battle,' murmured Isabella.

'Would've been better for him that he hadn't followed your King then, wouldn't it?' said the girl, but her voice was softer now.

Isabella sat up straight. 'Well, whatever you may think about it, I know what's right. I've got something very important to do. I have to take a message to the city of York, and I must get there as soon as possible. I shall ride at dawn.'

'Reckon you'd better get some sleep, then,' said the girl. 'That spot looks best – under the yew tree. It's dry and out of sight.'

'Thank you,' said Isabella haughtily. 'Goodnight.'

She wondered whether the girl would still be there when she woke the next morning, stiff and tired after a night on the hard, cold ground. Amid the rustling strangeness of the woods at night, she had felt very grateful for the girl's presence, just a few feet away from her, curled up under her cloak and breathing as easily as a baby in a cradle. Now, in the grey light of dawn, she saw the girl was still there, scraping over the ashes of the fire.

Isabella pushed her straggling hair back and attempted to brush off her muddy gown.

'I must go,' she announced. Then she felt rude, and added: 'Thank you for your help. My name is Isabella.'

'I'm Meg,' said the girl, not looking up.

Isabella went over to the pony, trying to ignore her aching legs. It felt odd to just go and leave the other girl here, all by herself in the forest. She wondered if she ought to ask her what she was going to do now, and whether she would be all right. Or ought she to make her a present of one of the coins she carried in her purse?

As she unhitched Brownie and made him ready to leave, he gave a little regretful whinny. She turned.

Meg had scattered the remains of the fire, and was now putting on her cloak again, as though she was ready to set off too.

'Are you leaving?' Isabella asked in surprise.

'That's right.'

'Where will you go?'

'Didn't you say you had a message to carry to York?'

Isabella stared at her for a moment. Meg's pale eyes stared back at her steadily.

'You want to *come with me*?'

'Well, I can't let you go off on your own, can I? You can't even cut the head off a rabbit right. Anyway, you're headed the wrong way.' Meg jerked her head in the opposite direction. 'York's over yonder.'

Isabella stood still, her hand on Brownie's bridle. Could she trust this girl? What if she were a spy for Cromwell's men? What if she were dangerous? She had said herself she was the daughter of a woman burned as a witch – and it was certain she cared nothing for the King. She hesitated, but then Meg mumbled:

'Besides, it's not as though I've anywhere else to be,' and gave her a quick, rueful smile.

Isabella felt a flicker of warmth ignite inside her. It was as bright as the little orange flame of her fire in the dark. Perhaps she did not know much about Meg, but there was no doubt that the forest felt more friendly with the other girl beside her. She turned to adjust the pony's girth. 'Well I suppose you can, if you like. I dare say Brownie could carry us both.'

She sprang up into the saddle, and Meg clambered up behind her. It was together that they went on, out of the clearing and into the forest, until they had disappeared between the trees.

Illustrations by Joel Stewart

The Journey Within

Annelise Heurtier

Aveleen kicked off her boots and let out a long sigh.

She had been walking for two days solid. How could it be that the Brown Mountain still seemed so far away? Had she taken a wrong turn and set off down one of those devious, false trails that send you round and round in circles?

Her body was slumped against the rock where she had stopped to rest. Her stomach churned with distress. Would she be back in time? Would she reward the trust that Celegorn had placed in her? Aveleen grabbed her waterskin and took three anguished gulps.

No matter how clear the signs, she still refused to accept that her father would soon be joining the Other Worlds. He may have been well past his 150th season, but he still seemed so… youthful. Not once had his body shown any sign of fatigue. Not once had his mind flagged in wisdom or constancy.

Yet the Tree had spoken. And the Tree was never wrong. A handful of its leaves had started to turn silver, a clear sign that for Celegorn the end was nigh. The time had come to find a new Chosen One to lead the people for the next cycle.

Many hopefuls had appeared in turn before the Tree. Like Lothar, the engraver's eldest son, who was said to have battled a Giant. Or Amæthon and Govannon, both born leaders of

men. And others still, all spurred on by their vigour and their determination to rule.

Yet for the first time in her people's history, the Tree had rejected each and every candidate.

Who was the unwitting Chosen One? Her friend Olirin, who had departed six moons ago to explore the kingdoms of the North? But he was just a child, too young to deem himself a leader. Would she find the answer at the top of the Brown Mountain, as her father had assured her?

Deep in thought, Aveleen pulled on her dust-covered boots and returned the waterskin to her pack. If she was going to daydream, she may as well do it on the move, otherwise she would stand no chance of being back before the last leaf on the Tree turned stiff with silver.

She was in a very strange place: a vast plain dotted with rocks, ash trees and sea buckthorn. It resembled her own land, but at the same time it was different. Two suns shone in the white sky.

The plants swayed despite the lack of any breeze. Where was she, exactly? She was not even sure if the region had a name. Celegorn had not given her many details. After spending a night of private contemplation beneath the Tree, he had simply announced:

'The Tree has spoken. The identity of the Chosen One is hidden in the lake at the crater of the Brown Mountain. I want you to make the journey.'

'In a lake?' Aveleen had asked. 'And why me?'

'It must be you, for I cannot trust the others not to bring back their own name.'

'Where is this lake? There is no such mountain in our land.'

'This is not a typical journey. The starting point is in the centre of the Tree. Go, get yourself ready!'

The sound of voices banished the image of Celegorn from her mind.

A few feet in front of Aveleen, the path was blocked by a pair of farmers in hot dispute. It was clear they were arguing over a bundle of wheat, which was at risk of being ripped to shreds before the matter was settled.

Where could these two have come from? Were they even real? The young girl brushed these questions aside and welcomed the chance to ask about her route. They did not seem in the least surprised at seeing the traveller.

'This is the last bundle,' he said, ignoring Aveleen's query entirely. 'I need it to bake bread. There's nothing sweeter than the sound of a loaf crisping up in the oven—'

'No, we need it to make *cake*, you stupid toad,' the woman protested. 'Then we can sell 'em, and for a good price!'

Aveleen looked at the couple for a moment. Standing side by side with their hands on their hips, tight-lipped and frowning heavily, they looked almost identical, like a mirror image of each other. They reminded her of someone, but she could not think who.

'Why don't you sow your grains of wheat?' Aveleen suggested after a moment's thought. 'With a bit of patience, you'll be able to make bread *and* cake!'

The man and the woman looked the girl up and down, as if seeing her in a fresh light.

'That's not a bad idea, you know. Wise words, young lady—'

'You should've thought of that!' the woman yelled at her husband.

'Same for you!'

As a fresh barrage of insults thundered from the odd couple, Aveleen decided to continue on her way, having lost all hope that they might come to her aid. But after only a few steps, the farmers caught up with her.

'Wait!' they shouted in perfect harmony. 'You're on a false trail. If you want to reach the Brown Mountain, you must not set foot on it. You have to walk alongside it, otherwise you'll never leave the valley.'

With the farmers' help, Aveleen eventually managed to abandon the path she had been stuck on for two days. But it was not long before she became thoroughly frustrated with her ascent of the Mountain. The slope was sheer and slippery, and the rocks kept scrambling underfoot to trip her up. The summit was still so far off… Would she be able to make it the whole way? She was not even sure how many days the journey was meant to last. 'It will take as much time as is necessary,' Celegorn had assured her. His answer had perplexed Aveleen. How could he say such a thing when the smallest delay might prevent her from bidding him farewell?

Aveleen hitched herself onto a small ledge as one of the suns was setting. Carved into the cliff face was a colossal bronze door, so high that it would have loomed over the heads of the Giants from her own land. She wondered what was inside. Had a people chosen to live in the cold, dark belly of the Mountain?

Aveleen ran her hands over the bronze before recoiling sharply. The door was opening in the middle.

'Welcome.'

A slender woman with big, shimmering eyes beckoned her inside. Aveleen let her bag slide to the ground and started forward, unable to offer any resistance.

All her doubts faded away as she followed in her hostess's wake.

Her first few paces left her stunned. She marvelled at the space, the light, the sky – how could all this exist inside a mountain? There was so much to admire that she found it hard to breathe. Trees, flowers, animals, buildings and people… wherever she laid her eyes, she was struck by the exquisite perfection around her. Never before had Aveleen experienced the profound, physical effect of ineffable beauty. The feeling overwhelmed her, almost sending her into disarray, as though her five senses had finally realized their true purpose.

She was led to a canopy that billowed in the gentle breeze. Inside, the woman gave her garments whose colours did not exist in her land. She then presented her with all manner of unfamiliar dishes, like desserts that were somehow both piping-hot and icy-cold, or biscuits whose texture and flavour shifted with every bite, one second as dense as a storm cloud, the next as light as sea foam.

Aveleen felt she could spend an entire lifetime exploring the wonders of this place and still not skim the surface. Time seemed to stand still. She stayed there for several days, maybe months, until the woman with the crystalline eyes returned to her side.

'Tomorrow, we shall organize a ceremony,' she said. 'You are to become one of us. If you live with us for ever more, you will not know pain or suffering, you...'

Aveleen let herself be cradled by the woman's words. Her face was so reassuring, the tone of her voice so enchanting. Again there was a certain familiarity. The woman reminded her of someone, but she could not think who. Her face evoked a vague memory of Celegorn, which stirred Aveleen from her slumber. How could she have forgotten her mission? They were relying on her.

She decided to leave the City.

Aveleen had gone for several days without any boots. The Mountain had rallied in its efforts to frustrate her progress, and now her soles had given way to the rocks, glaciers and deserts that she had crossed. Deserts halfway up a mountain? Aveleen had needed to summon all her reserves of energy to go on. She had lost count of how many times she thought she might die of thirst, only to stumble on a drop of water in a plant she knew from her own land. More than once she had considered turning back to the City.

What if she found nothing at the end?

But Aveleen remained resolute. She reached the crater of the Brown Mountain one cold day at dawn. She had walked through the night, unable to focus on anything except putting one foot in front of the other.

The plain below was gleaming in the setting light of the twin suns. It seemed so very distant. How many months had passed since she had left? How many green leaves could there still be on the Tree?

Aveleen batted these thoughts aside. Just ahead, the lake in the mountain's crater sparkled like a patch of sky that had fallen from the heavens. She felt her heart pounding as she scrambled down the last of the gentle slope, her eyes never leaving the lake. A few steps away, there was a fearsome rumble, and the earth began to shake beneath her feet, causing her to sink to her knees. When she opened her eyes, she saw before her a vast chasm blocking her way to the lake. After a moment's stunned silence, a mighty wave of anger tore through the young girl. Why this final obstacle when she was just feet away from completing her quest? Aveleen flung back her head and let out a howl of rage and bewilderment.

A swoosh of wings cut short her cries. Aveleen turned to see a crow staring at her without flinching, its feathers lustrous in the evening light. Straight away the bird inspired an intense dislike in her. Something in its eyes made her deeply suspicious. Yet again, however, the crow reminded her of someone… Why was she so utterly incapable of establishing who?

'Why didn't you just pick the name of the Chosen One yourself, you idiot?' the crow cawed. 'You would have spared yourself the journey. Look at you, all covered in muck. I don't know if the villagers will laugh or cry when you tell them about your miserable failure.'

The crow still stared at Aveleen with its beady, mocking eyes.

'Unless… unless I go on your behalf? Here, give me your gold necklace and I'll take care of it.'

Aveleen was so incredulous she wanted to burst out laughing. She did not believe the crow's words for a second.

A large golden ladybird chose that very moment to land on Aveleen's hand. The girl watched as it took off again and settled a few inches from the precipice. Then something inexplicable happened. Instead of making a turn, the ladybird carried on straight ahead, before zigzagging across the void. At first, Aveleen thought her weary body was making her see things. But the proof was undeniable; as clear as day, the ladybird was standing in the middle of the chasm.

Ignoring the crow's gesticulations, Aveleen approached the gap and, still on her knees, started tapping it with her knuckle.

It was quite incredible… she could see the chasm, but in several places, she felt firm ground too.

'Is it your hands or your eyes that deceive you?' the crow snickered again and again. Aveleen tried to ignore it, seeking refuge in her thoughts.

The Tree had protected her people since time immemorial. It was unthinkable that she had been led to a dead end. There had to be a way to reach the lake. There had to be.

Still lost in thought and overcome with nerves, Aveleen started distractedly ripping handfuls of wild grass from the ground. It was only when she saw the two piles that had formed either side of her that she had the idea.

She stood up slowly and threw the first lot into the precipice. The grass marked out a path.

Aveleen shoved the rest of it into her leather pack. Her heart racing, she placed a foot on the green walkway as the crow flew off with a squawk.

There it was.

The Lake sparkled like a silver fish. Aveleen caught sight of her reflection in the mercury water. She instinctively brought a hand to her cheek. She seemed different. And not just because of the mud smeared across her face.

As Aveleen entered the cold water, her clothes drifted around her like flailing, broken wings. She emerged from the piercing depths hours later with a sense of emptiness. There was nothing at the bottom of the lake.

Nothing.

Beneath the algae

there was nothing but

fine sand.

On the bank, Aveleen curled up to regain some warmth. She fell into a deep sleep, oblivious to the roiling sky over her head that was about to engulf her.

* * *

Aveleen woke with a jolt and immediately made herself remember. The Lake. She must have missed a clue, some stone buried in the silt, or a piece of wood that had gone unnoticed with the name engraved on it.

She opened her eyes abruptly, but the scream she wanted to unleash stayed lodged in her throat.

What was she doing in her house?

Celegorn was facing her, hunched over more than ever. Old age had suddenly caught up with him; his body seemed completely dilapidated. Aveleen felt tears at her eyes. She was not sure if it was sorrow at seeing her father in that state, joy at being reunited with him or fury that she had come home without a name.

'Tell me what you saw up there,' Celegorn said, anticipating his daughter's flood of questions.

With a sense of urgency, Aveleen disappeared into the depths of her memory. The crow, the chasm, the bottom of the lake, the cold, the weeds.

She knew she had been wrong to fall asleep on the shore. Could she return there now?

'So you did not see a single face?' Celegorn asked.

Aveleen shook her head vigorously. Apart from her reflection in the surface, there had been nothing.

Her father was now giving her an unusual look.

Her... reflection?

Her... reflection?

Aveleen felt as if the blood was draining from her body. Yes, she had seen a face in the Lake.

Her own.

She was numb. Could she be the Chosen One?

'I have always believed in you,' Celegorn continued. 'But when it became clear that you would not offer yourself to the Tree, I knew I had to help you realize who you are, who you have been since you were young. I watched you throughout your journey. You showed wisdom, loyalty and great courage. You were able to make difficult decisions. Do you remember?'

Memories from the journey jostled about in her mind, tracing the outline of a gigantic puzzle whose final image she already knew.

'So this quest was your idea? The Tree never said that the name was at the summit? But if that's the case, how can you be sure that I am the Chosen One?'

'There is not much time,' Celegorn said in his quiet voice. 'You have been gone seven days, and only a few leaves remain on the Tree. If you feel it within you, then come.'

'But wait! Was it real?'

'Does that matter?' Celegorn asked.

Aveleen felt a surge of strength well up inside her. Now she realized what lay behind the glimmers of recognition in those she had met on her journey within. They were her dark, disloyal, weak sides, and she had triumphed over them.

Aveleen passed through the whispering crowd. No woman had ever put herself forward.

But when the Tree, their protector, embraced the girl in its branches, illuminating her with a silver halo, no one could question the identity of their new guide.

Aveleen looked up at them and smiled.

Now she knew that it was her.

And she was ready.

Translated from the French by Sam Gordon

Illustrations by Ian Beck

ABOUT THE AUTHORS

Alaine Agirre was born in Bermeo, a small fishing village on the coast of Bizkaia, in Spain, but now lives in San Sebastian, where she spends her free time with her two greyhounds, her flute and her piano. Although she studied Physics and Basque Philology, she has always had a passion for writing, and that is what she mostly devotes herself to now. Six of her children's books have been published within the last few years as well as two books of adult fiction – all written in her native Basque.

Andri Antoniou was born in Cyprus in 1980. She graduated from the Department of Primary Education of the University of Cyprus and is currently working as a teacher. Her first middle-grade novel was published in 2012 under the title *Beladomagnitis (Trouble Magnet)* and received the National Prize Award for Literature for Older Children and Teenagers for 2012. Her second middle-grade novel was published in 2013 under the title *Penelope* and was included in the shortlist for the National Prize Award for Literature for 2013. Her third-middle grade novel under the title *Kardia pano se rodes (Heart on Wheels)* was published in October 2016. All three books were published by Psichogios Publications. She has been awarded three times in a prestigious children's literature competition organized by the Women's Literary Team of Greece.

Stefan Bachmann was born in Colorado and spent most of his childhood in Switzerland, in a very old house next to a forest. At the age of eleven, he entered the Zürich Conservatory in piano and composition, and is currently preparing to graduate from the Zürich University of Arts with a degree in modern music. He is also the author of several books, the first of which was published when he was nineteen years old. His books have been translated into eight languages and have been named, among others, a *Publishers Weekly* Best Book of the Year, a *New York Times* Editor's Choice and a VOYA Best Science Fiction and Fantasy Book of the Year for Children.

Ævar Þór Benediktsson is an actor and author, best known in Iceland for his work as Ævar the Scientist (in TV, radio and books) and for his best-selling *Your Very Own* series of books, where the reader takes an active role in shaping the storyline. Ævar has won several awards for his work, including the Icelandic Children's Book Awards, the Bookseller's Awards, three Edda awards for his TV show and a special award, from the ministry of culture and education, in recognition of his contribution to the Icelandic language.

Laura Dockrill is an award-winning British author and illustrator. Her *Darcy Burdock* series has been short-listed for the Waterstones Book of The Year Prize and both *Darcy Burdock* and *Lorali* have been nominated for the Carnegie Medal. Her previous works *Mistakes in the Background*, *Ugly Shy Girl* and *Echoes* earned her many plaudits. She has performed works on BBC Radio 1 through 6, on programmes including *Woman's Hour*, *Open Book* and *Blue Peter*. Laura is on the advisory panel at the Ministry Of Stories, and has judged many literary prizes including the John Betjeman Poetry Prize, the BBC National Short Story Prize and the BAFTA Children's Prize.

Ludovic Flamant was born in Namur, Belgium, in 1978 and won the Prix International Jeunes Auteurs (International Price for Young Writers) in 1995 and 1996. He wrote a play called *Peep Show* in 2002 and the novel *Être Vera* in 2003. In 2005, he published his first children's book, *Chafi*, and since then he has devoted himself to children's books. He occasionally translates books into French, such as *The Gashlycrumb Tinies* by Edward Gorey, for example.

ABOUT THE AUTHORS

Annelise Heurtier was born in 1979 near Lyon in France. So far she has written about twenty books, for a broad audience, ranging from young children to teenagers and young adults. Some of her books have been translated into Italian, Spanish, Korean and Chinese. Her best-seller *Sweet Sixteen* (published by Casterman in 2013) is based on the real story of the Nine of Little Rock who have fought for racial integration. Already considered a classic of young-adult literature, it has been much praised by the critics and was nominated for about thirty literary awards.

David Machado was born in Portugal in 1978. He published his first children's book, *A Noite dos Animais Inventados*, in 2006, after winning the Prémio Branquinho da Fonseca for children's literature. Since then he has published eight other children books, most of them with great critical and public acclaim. He won the Prémio SPA for best Portuguese children's book with *O Tubarão na Banheira*. He has also published three novels and a collection of short stories. His novel *Índice Médio de Felicidade* won the European Union Prize for Literature in 2015 and is now being turned into a film. His books have been translated into more than ten languages.

Maria Parr was born in Norway in 1981 and has a Master's degree in Nordic languages and literature. As well as being a writer, she is a part-time teacher. She grew up in Fiskå, a little village on the west coast of Norway, and has recently moved back there with her family. She published *Waffle Hearts* at the age of twenty-four. Norway's main TV channel NRK made it into a TV series in November 2011, and the book was nominated for the Brage Award. Parr's second children's novel, *Tonje Glimmerdal* (2009), is considered to be her definitive breakthrough. It won the Brage Prize for the best children's book in 2009 and the Critics' Prize 2009 in Norway, as well as the LUCHS-preis, for the best children's book in Germany 2010. Both books have been translated into several languages.

Dy Plambeck was born in 1980 in the northern part of Zealand, Denmark. In 2004 she graduated from the Danish Writer's School, and in 2005 her first book, *Tales from Bure Lake*, was published. Since then she has published the novels *Texas Rose* (2008), *Godfather* (2011) and *Mikael* (2014), and the children's books *The Bloomtown Kids* (vols. 1–12, 2011–15) and *The Hill of Dreams* (2008). Her work has garnered critical and popular acclaim. She has received several awards for her writing, such as the Danish Academy's debut prize (2006), the Art State Foundation three-year grant (2006), the Jytte Borberg Prize (2011) and the Henri Nathansen Prize (2012).

Katherine Rundell is a Fellow in English Literature at All Souls College in Oxford; her doctorate was on John Donne, Latin satire and Renaissance forgery. Her first book, *The Girl Savage*, won the *Boston Globe* Horn Book award in America; her second, *Rooftoppers*, won the *Blue Peter* Prize and the Waterstones Children's Book Award, and is translated into fifteen languages. Her most recent book, *The Wolf Wilder*, is about the Russian revolution, ballet and wolves.

Nataly Savina was born in Riga in Latvia, spent some of her teenage years in Helsinki and moved to southern Germany, where she finished school. Then she studied Arts and Cultural Sciences in Hildesheim, and scriptwriting at the Berlin Film Academy. Since 2008, she has been working as a freelance writer for cinema and television, as well as on her novels. She lives in Berlin with her partner and their three kids.

Aline Sax is a Flemish author of children's and young adult novels. She has a PhD in History and currently works as a historian and novelist. She wrote her first book when she was fifteen, about two German child soldiers at the Normandy beaches in June 1944. So far she has written fifteen novels, most of them set in the past and capturing a wide range of themes and historical periods. Her books are written in Dutch, and have been translated into German, Danish,

Swedish, French, Korean, Arabic and English. She has been nominated for and won several literary prizes.

Jana Šrámková discovered her passion for writing at a theological seminary. She began to read obsessively and decided to pursue a Master in Literature and Creative Writing. During her studies she published her first short novel, which was awarded the Jiří Orten Prize. Only after that was she finally able to publish her first real manuscript which had been written for children. She finished a personal fragmentary prose about her grandma, and last year she published two picture books. She is working on her PhD at the Theatre Faculty of the Academy of Performing Arts in her native Prague, where she lives with her husband, three kids and two cats.

Maria Turtschaninoff is a Swedish-speaking Finn who has been writing fairy tales from the age of five. After a brief stint as a journalist for a few years, Turtschaninoff debuted in 2007 with a middle-grade portal fantasy and has since published four more novels, all YA fantasy. *Maresi* won the prestigious Finlandia Junior Award in 2014, has been sold to eighteen territories and been getting rave reviews in publications such as *The Guardian*, *The Financial Times*, *The Telegraph*, *The Daily Mail* and *Metro*. Her latest novel, *Naondel*, was released in Finland and Sweden in the autumn of 2016 and in the UK in April 2017.

Anna Woltz, who was born in the Netherlands in 1981, has written twenty-one books for young readers. Some of her books are adventurous stories for ten-year-olds, others are challenging young-adult novels. Her books have been translated into nine languages (English, German, French, Slovenian, Norwegian, Danish, Hungarian, Japanese and Taiwanese) and have won several prizes. Woltz was first published when she was fifteen years old: she wrote a weekly column about her high school life for a national newspaper. She studied History at Leyden University and is now a full-time writer.

Katherine Woodfine is the author of the best-selling *Sinclair's Mysteries* series, beginning with *The Clockwork Sparrow*, which was shortlisted for the Waterstones Children's Book Prize, longlisted for the Branford Boase Award and nominated for the CILIP Carnegie Medal. Until 2015 she worked for reading charity BookTrust on projects including the Children's Laureate. She now combines writing with reviewing children's books, presenting *Down the Rabbit Hole*, a monthly radio show and podcast discussing children's literature, and organising YALC, an annual event for thousands of young-adult readers. Her latest book is *The Painted Dragon*.

ABOUT THE TRANSLATORS

Avgi Daferera is a literary translator working from Greek into English and vice versa. She holds an MA in Writing from the University of Warwick and an MA in Literary Translation from the University of East Anglia. In 2016 she joined the Greek Ersilia Literary Agency, where she works as the Children's Rights Assistant.

Amaia Gabantxo is a writer, flamenco singer and literary translator specialized in Basque literature. She teaches creative writing at the University of Chicago, and has over twenty translated works to her name. A pilgrim soul, she has lived, worked, studied, published and performed on both sides of the Atlantic.

Roland Glasser translates literary and genre fiction from French, as well as art, travel and assorted non-fiction. His translation of Fiston Mwanza Mujila's *Tram 83* won the Etisalat Prize for Literature 2016 and was nominated for the Man Booker International Prize and the Best Translated Book Award.

Sam Gordon is a London-based translator from the French and Spanish. He has translated work by authors including Timothée de Fombelle, Karim Miské, Pierre Lemaitre, Sophie Hénaff, Matthieu Ricard and Nicolás Di Candia. His translations have appeared in *Asymptote*, *The White Review* and *Palabras Errantes*.

Fiona Graham grew up in rural Herefordshire and Kenya, before studying German and French at Oxford. Since then she has lived in the Netherlands, Luxembourg and Belgium, with a spell in Nicaragua. Her first book-length translation, from Swedish, came out in early 2017.

Lucy Greaves translates from Portuguese and Spanish. She won the 2013 Harvill Secker Young Translators' Prize and in 2014 was Translator in Residence at the Free Word Centre in London. Her latest translation, María Angélica Bosco's *Death Going Down,* is published by Pushkin Press. She lives in Bristol, UK.

Rosie Hedger is a freelance translator from Norwegian into English. Her translation of Agnes Ravatn's *The Bird Tribunal* won an English PEN Translates Award in 2016, with the book selected for BBC Radio 4's *Book at Bedtime.* Having lived in Norway, Sweden and Denmark, Rosie is now based in the UK.

Meg Matich is a Reykjavik-based translator and a current Fulbright grantee. She has received grants and fellowships from PEN America, the DAAD, the Banff Centre, the Icelandic Literature Centre and Columbia University. She is currently assisting with the 2017 Reykjavik Literary Festival.

A.A. Prime (or Annie to her friends) is a freelance literary translator specializing in fantasy and YA fiction, which she is quite certain is the best job in the world. Since her MA in Translation from UCL she has translated two novels by Maria Turtschaninoff: *Maresi* (nominated for the 2017 Carnegie Medal) and *Naondel.*

Guy Puzey is from Scotland, just a short swim away from Norway. He has been translating Norwegian literature since 2006, having studied the language at the University of Edinburgh, where he is now Lecturer in Scandinavian Studies. He likes translating books about waffles and people who know how to ski.

ABOUT THE TRANSLATORS

Laura Watkinson studied medieval and modern languages at Oxford, and taught English around the world before returning to the UK and completing a postgraduate course in literary translation at UCL. She now lives in Amsterdam and is a full-time translator from Dutch, Italian and German. Her work on children's books has won her the Vondel Prize (for Tonke Dragt's *The Letter for the King*) and multiple Batchelder Awards.

Alex Zucker has translated novels by Czech authors Jáchym Topol, Petra Hůlová, Tomáš Zmeškal, Magdaléna Platzová, Josef Jedlička, Heda Margolius Kovály, Patrik Ouředník and Miloslava Holubová. In 2010 he received the ALTA National Translation Award. He lives in Brooklyn, New York.

ABOUT THE ILLUSTRATORS

Ian Beck is a British author and illustrator renowned for his series *Tom Trueheart* (translated into seventeen countries), as well as his many award-winning picture books, including *The Teddy Robber*. He has also collaborated with authors such as Berlie Doherty and Philip Pullman.

Lilian Brøgger is a prize-winning Danish illustrator. So far she has illustrated around 200 children's books, and has been published in eighteen countries. Lilian's work is regularly exhibited in her homeland and abroad, and she also teaches at international workshops.

Ross Collins has illustrated over 100 books and written a good dozen, such as *The Elephantom* and *There's a Bear on My Chair*, winning many awards along the way. His work is published in over twenty countries. Ross lives in Scotland where he likes to swing precariously backwards on chairs.

Benji Davies is a British illustrator, author and animation director. He has worked on an array of projects, from picture books and animated films to music videos and commercials. With his books now published around the world, Benji has won many awards, both in the UK and internationally. He lives in London with his wife Nina.

Anna Höglund, considered one of Sweden's foremost illustrators, has collaborated with authors such as Ulf Stark and Barbro Lindgren. She also writes her own books. She has received many prestigious awards from around the globe, including the Deutscher Jugendliteraturpreis and the Astrid Lindgren Prize.

Neal Layton's studio walls are covered with pictures, drawings, scribbles, badges, photos, posters, packaging and anything else that he finds inspiring. There he writes and illustrates his award-winning stories. He lives in Portsmouth, England, and he enjoys the seaside.

Barbara Nascimbeni studied illustration in Milan, Italy, and Darmstadt, Germany. She works with international publishers from England, France, Italy, Germany and Korea, and her books have been translated in many languages. She lives and works in Hamburg, Germany and Sorède, France.

Charlotte Pardi was born in a little village in Jutland, Denmark. She graduated in 1998 from the Kolding School of Design. Since then, she has worked as an illustrator for the prestigious Danish weekly, *Weekendavisen*. She has also illustrated more than forty picture books for children.

Moni Port is an award-winning German illustrator, writer and cover designer. She is one of the founders of LABOR studio collective, along with Anke Kuhl and Philip Waechter. She lives in Frankfurt, Germany. Her books have been translated in many languages.

Chris Riddell is the creator of a wide range of books, which have won many illustration awards including the UNESCO Prize, the Greenaway Medal (twice) and the Hay Festival Medal for Illustration. In 2015 he was appointed Children's Laureate in the UK.

Tony Ross is one of the most popular children's book illustrators. He has worked on more than 800 books, by authors such as Roald Dahl, Michael Palin and

Paula Danziger. He also finds time to write and illustrate his own books. Tony never thought he'd be an artist, but "fell into it" when his dreams of being a cowboy fell through.

Axel Scheffler was born in Hamburg, Germany, in 1957. He moved to the UK in 1982 to study visual communications at Bath Academy of Art and has worked as a freelance illustrator in London since 1987. He is best known for his collaborations with Julia Donaldson, such as *The Gruffalo*, and his *Pip and Posy* series.

Kamila Slocinska is a Danish-Polish illustrator, author and artist. Since the beginning of her career in 2011, Kamila has illustrated more than ten children's books and digital interactive stories, written by some of Denmark's most acclaimed writers. She also writes and illustrates her own books. Her work has been published in Denmark, Norway, Germany and Hong Kong.

Joel Stewart is a British illustrator known internationally for his *Dexley Bexley* picture books. He has also illustrated the words of others including Julia Donaldson, Carol Ann Duffy and Michael Rosen. His work has won many prizes. He created and directed the hit children's animation series *The Adventures of Abney & Teal* and is also a musician, collecting and playing increasingly odd instruments.

Adam Stower is a Brighton-based British illustrator. He has won many prizes for his work in the picture-book world (notably for *Bottoms Up* by Jeanne Willis and *Slam!*, which he wrote and illustrated). Adam is also well-known as a black-and-white illustrator for chapter books, bringing stories to life in a few pen strokes.

Cato Thau-Jensen is a Danish illustrator who made his debut with the picture book *Og så er det godnat!* (*And Now Good Night!*, 1995), and has since worked with Kim Fupz Aakeson, among other authors. He is a part of the generation of "young wild" illustrators to come out of the Kolding Design School during the 1990s. He has both written and illustrated the books *Kanuld på Mammutsletten* (*Kanuld on the Mammoth Plains*, 2012) and the autobiographical *Et hjem med gevær* (*A Home with a Shotgun*, 2007).

Philip Waechter is one of Germany's best-known illustrators. His children's books have met with international success, most notably *ME!*, published by Random House. He lives in Frankfurt, is a member of the LABOR collective and loves football.

ABOUT THE AARHUS 39

Aarhus 39 is a collection of the best emerging writers for young people from across wider Europe. The authors have been selected by three of Europe's much-loved writers – Kim Fupz Aakeson (Denmark), Ana Cristina Herreros (Spain) and Matt Haig (UK) – and commissioned to write an original story to the theme of 'Journey'.

The writers are invited to spend five days in Aarhus visiting schools and taking part in the International Children's Literature Hay Festival in Aarhus which runs 26–29th October 2017.

The 39 selected writers are:

1. Ævar Þór Benediktsson – Iceland
2. Alaine Agirre – Spain
3. Aline Sax – Belgium
4. Ana Pessoa – Portugal
5. Andri Antoniou – Cyprus
6. Anna Woltz – Netherlands
7. Annelise Heurtier – France
8. Annette Münch – Norway
9. B.R. Collins – UK
10. Cathy Clement – Luxembourg
11. Cornelia Travnicek – Austria
12. David Machado – Portugal
13. Dy Plambeck – Denmark
14. Elisabeth Steinkellner – Austria

15. Endre Lund Eriksen – Norway
16. Finn-Ole Heinrich – Germany
17. Frida Nilsson – Sweden
18. Gideon Samson – Netherlands
19. Inna Manakhova – Russia
20. Jana Šrámková – Czech Republic
21. Katherine Rundell – UK
22. Katherine Woodfine – UK
23. Laura Dockrill – UK
24. Laura Gallego – Spain
25. Ludovic Flamant – Belgium
26. Maria Parr – Norway
27. Maria Turtschaninoff – Finland
28. Michaela Holzinger – Austria
29. Nataly Elisabeth Savina – Germany
30. Nina Elisabeth Grøntvedt – Norway
31. Peder Frederik Jensen – Denmark
32. Salla Simukka – Finland
33. Sandrine Kao – France
34. Sanne Munk Jensen – Denmark
35. Sarah Crossan – Ireland
36. Sarah Engell – Denmark
37. Stefan Bachmann – Switzerland
38. Stefanie de Velasco – Germany
39. Victor Dixen – France

For more information, please visit
www.hayfestival.com/aarhus39

COPYRIGHT INFORMATION